RAVEN GAMES

Raven Games

by

PAUL O. INGRAM

RESOURCE *Publications* · Eugene, Oregon

RAVEN GAMES

Resource Publications
An Imprint of Wipf and Stock Publishers
199 W. 8th Ave., Suite 3
Eugene, OR 97401

www.wipfandstock.com

PAPERBACK ISBN: 979-8-3852-1841-7
HARDCOVER ISBN: 979-8-3852-1842-4
EBOOK ISBN: 979-8-3852-1843-1

05/24/24

I

The phone rang at 8:15 p.m. I was working late at the university on chores neglected for too long: churning out year-end reports and putting the final touches on a survey of the bear population in the North Cascades. In early June life is full of deadlines for untenured university instructors. Mostly it involves paid administrators crunching numbers on computers to cover their collective backsides. Most are like the rear area officers I knew in Vietnam. I have a theory about university administrators and rear area military officers. Being one would make a son of a bitch of Jesus Christ.

At the time I was standing at my office window seven stories up in the natural sciences building daydreaming about ravens and grizzly bears. The saw-toothed ridges of the Olympic Mountains west of Puget Sound were backlit by the last red glow of the sun setting below the horizon. In the fading daylight below the university, Seattle was spread out like a lumpy concrete slab toward Elliot Bay. The June air was unusually dry and shimmering with the last embers of sunset blending with the city's lights and the first pale radiance of moonrise, a full moon rolling on the darkening sky above the city like a white mask.

The phone rang and pushed my senses back into my office. "Yes?" I said flatly.

"I have a person-to-person call for Professor David Elwin from a Jamie Bear Mother's Daughter."

The operator's voice sounded computerized and reminded me of the way bananas taste. "This is Elwin," I replied curtly as I sat behind my desk and tried to picture the last time I saw her. I mostly remembered how, when she straightened out my tie, she always straightened out much more.

"How are you, David?" Her voice was husky as if she breathed words into the receiver the way she breathed music into her reed flute—another memory that made me feel as hollow as a broken drum.

"Well enough," I answered. "Didn't think I'd be hearing from you again. I've missed you."

I knew it was a mistake as soon as I said it. "Don't start," I silently scolded myself. "When a thing is over, it's over. Say something else."

"How's Born of Songs?"

"Born of Songs still gets around," she answered cautiously. "It's harder now. He says he's looking for a good day to die."

"That's called suicide," I replied nervously. "It's even against the law in some places. Still doesn't like his Anglo name?"

"Grandfather is a Haida shaman. He wears any name he wishes, and he can choose his day to die."

Her reply was defiant, and my spine stiffened as I listened to her breathing over the hissing connection. "I hope your grandfather lives for another fifty years. If anyone deserves long life, it's Born of Songs."

"He's your grandfather too. You've been adopted. Have you forgotten so soon? Besides, it's not always that life is too short. It may be too long." Her voice cracked to a whisper. "You can lie to yourself about anything, except death."

She paused and waited for me to answer. There was something in her voice I hadn't heard before. I wasn't sure what it was, but I didn't like it.

"Grandfather needs you," she finally said. "Can you meet me in Ketchikan, and I mean soon?"

It was fear. She tried to cover it and couldn't. That in itself was unusual. The granddaughter of a Haida shaman and proud of it, Jamie Bear Mother's Daughter incarnated every stereotype of Indian women known to white men and women. She knew all about these stereotypes, but she played roles anyway as if white expectations were a ceremonial mask to put on or take off as circumstances demanded. It was always hard to know her real feelings because she hid them behind these masks. It was easier to read the painted figures on a Haida totem pole than her facial expressions or tone of voice.

"Can you be more specific? This is short notice, and Ketchikan's a long way from Seattle. Hell, Ketchikan's a long way from anywhere. Besides, I'm supposed to be in Yellowstone next week counting grizz."

Her voice faltered, like someone looking over her shoulder while talking to see if the coast is clear. "It's not too far for us, and there's plenty of grizz to count around here."

"Listen, Jamie, this isn't a good time because—"

"Are you coming or not?" she demanded.

"All right, what's going on? What are you afraid of?" I remembered my own fear when that damned trickster, Raven, followed me to Vietnam. I hadn't heard his voice since, but I had an uneasy certainty he was about to call again.

"It's Jonathan. He's gone crazy."

"Nothing new about that. Your brother's been certifiably insane since Vietnam. Hell, everyone who was there went crazy, especially me. Why should Jonathan be any different?'

"He's stopped drinking."

I pushed back in my chair. "That's not good."

"Damned straight it's not. The only time he isn't crazy is when he's drunk. You know that. His demons come out when he's sober." She paused, the way she always did to give important words time to sink in. "He's been on the wagon for six weeks."

"Damn it! Your brother's calling in my marker and you're doing it for him."

"It's time. Please get up here. Jonathan needs you. So does Grandfather."

"All right. Sit tight. I'll meet you at the ferry dock in Prince Rupert in three days."

"Thank you, David," she sighed. "I've missed you."

When the university shuts down in three-week hibernation before the summer quarter, thirty thousand students disappear the way a magician vanishes from a sealed box. Only a few faculty and administrators hang around finishing semester-ending chores, along with graduate students mutating into zombies by their research, staying holed up in libraries and labs like cloistered monks and nuns. They are not part of the living even when the university is operating at full tilt, but more like the living dead whose spooky presence haunts the early summer solitude of the place.

The next morning, I drafted resignation letters to the university and the US Forest Service and cleaned out my desk. My summer research in Yellowstone National Park was a population study of grizzly bears and was now out of the question. But it was necessary research, and I didn't like giving it up. The Yellowstone bear count was increasing as the grizz moved outside the Park's boundaries. This meant more unregulated human contact and trouble. Bears caught on ranch land were either shot, poisoned, or occasionally blown up, mostly illegally. Law-and-order ranchers get very creative in their application of the law when bears do what comes naturally and eat their stock. But it's a matter of profit and loss, not law, and the grizz always lose.

Except for Peggy Harrison, I was alone. She was a department secretary, but also much more. I handed her the draft of my letter to be retyped as I filled her in.

"Sounds bad," she said. "You could be in for a world of hurt."

Tall and blond, in her midforties, Peggy knew about men who had fought in Vietnam. The war had mutated her husband from a gentle human being into a drug-abusing wifebeater. After a year back in the world, he killed a prostitute in a sleazy upstairs room over a waterfront bar. He still claims he doesn't remember doing it. But the poor bastard will spend the rest of his life in the state penitentiary at Walla Walla trying to. Peggy filed for divorce after the trial.

"I'll be careful," I said coyly. "Just type the letter and sign my name. I'll mail it on the way out."

"It'll be ready." She started typing. "Better take protection."

"Thank you, Mother," I teased. "I always take my .45 pistol and my .30-30 Winchester into grizzly country."

She stopped typing and fixed her gaze on the keyboard. "Grizzlies are the least of your problems," she said flatly. She resumed typing. "Get along. I'll mail it for you. Stay safe."

Peggy Harrison was one tough woman and I deeply admired her for it, a realistic cynic who never asked for kindness nor gave it cheaply.

2

There are three ways to get to Ketchikan from Seattle. The fastest way is by jet, but this was out. I needed time to sort things out before I got there. The Alaska-Marine Highway System runs a two-day service from Puget Sound north between Vancouver Island and the Canadian mainland through the Strait of Georgia to Ketchikan and the Queen Charlottes. I decided against that too. I didn't want that much time with anything to do except think. So, I drove. It was a matter of self-preservation. The mind is often as shapeless as silly putty. Vietnam and Raven taught me that. Only one thing was certain. I didn't comprehend the dark forces I was moving into, except that they were waiting for me like hungry ghosts. I drove because I think best when I'm doing something.

Seattle to Ketchikan through Prince Rupert takes three days of hard driving through country that's a frontier full of Scandinavianly white people whose God commanded them to work hard, play hard, multiply hard, and dominate the land. Which they did with a technological vengeance grounded in aggressive ignorance of the dark side of the landscape, an Indian side filled with spirits and history pushed into unconsciousness to keep white fantasies from turning into nightmares. To white settlers, frontiers meant new possibilities. But the native people inhabiting the land know how the forces sculpting it are ancient and unpredictable. Which is why they held on and never left.

Interstate 5 between Seattle and the Canadian border bisects Puget Sound and the North Cascades with a corridor of monuments to Anglo-American fantasies: the high rises of Seattle and the Space Needle, the campus of the University of Washington, the Boeing plant of Everett, all glued together by the concrete and steel of urban sprawl. Road signs, campers, sport cars, people on the go, on the make, earning money, raising Cain. Rich people, poor people, in-between people. Handsome men with sexy women wearing skimpy dresses. Old men and women watching them and wishing they were young again. Parents worried about their children's futures. Children swimming mindlessly like dolphins in the present. They all seemed incorporeal, disembodied flashes of light. It's a shock to be surrounded by ghosts driving cars and trucks in broad daylight at high speed on an interstate. And that you are one of them.

Above Bellingham, the urban sprawl begins to thin as green begins to return to the land. From the turnoff at State Highway 539, the road runs through miles of berry fields more or less straight to Lynden, where it meets Highway 546 at Sumas and crosses the Canadian border. I decided to stop for the night in Hope, British Columbia, two and a half hours from Sumas. Around 10:00 p.m. I pulled off the road behind a grove of red cedars north of town, ate, and settled into the night's silences.

There are all kinds of silence and each means something different. There is silence before and after a thunderstorm. There is the silence of war and the numb silence after a firefight. I have heard them all. There is also an interior silence that wells up from memories and recollection, beyond description and unconnected with what we can see in the external world, a silence no one else hears when you hear it. I never know when I'll hear this silence. The first time was in the isolation of Born of Song's cabin. It still rings in my mind like a bell's echo. Always just before Raven calls my name. Is this a dream? What the hell is the line between dreams and reality? I hadn't heard this silence for a long time—not since I got back from Nam. But it came again that night outside of Hope.

3

Jonathan Blue Heron hated being Indian. It took me a long time to figure out why. It was the first thing we talked about when I met him in 1969. "It's a damned drag," he said. "Indians are always dirt poor with no place to go." It was our first day of basic training at Fort Ord. We were in the Army barber shop undergoing the process of transformation into soldiers. The draft had snatched me like a cat burglar from my third year at Stanford where I was majoring in anthropology. I hated the Army for disrupting my life. I wasn't alone. Everyone in my training company hated the Army. Except Jonathan. He loved the Army. Looking back, maybe this and the fact that I studied Indian culture at Stanford made him an object of my curiosity. He was a powerful man physically, but it wasn't just his size. It was the way he moved, always efficient, with no wasted energy, relaxed yet always alert, guided by hunter's eyes that never missed movement.

"There's more grizzly bears than people," he said as the Army barber mowed skin-deep strips through his shoulder-length, jet-black hair. "Ketchikan's the nearest town. Isn't much, though. It's always raining. Ever been there?"

I told him I'd only read about the place and that it didn't sound like any place I wanted to go.

"Can't remember the last time that town saw the sun," he said.

I tried to be sociable and laughed as I stared at the final lengths of his hair falling to the floor. "Sounds like the end of the world."

"Yeah, and the Army's my ticket out."

"What's there to do in Ketchikan?"

"Mostly bar hop. Maybe shoot a little pool and get drunk. Nothing crazier than a drunk Indian." He stood up when the barber finished and looked at his reflection in the mirror. "Sometimes pick up a woman. But the pickings are slim as hell for Indians. He turned and grinned. "I do believe you're next, white boy."

"Seems to me they'd be especially slim for a bald Indian," I said. The barber motioned me to take Jonathan's place. "You plan on being a thirty-year man?"

In the mirror, I could see his dark brown eyes glued on the back of my head and his mouth curled up in a grin. "Hell no. I'm doing my four and that's it." Baldness exaggerated his flat nose, high cheeks, and slightly protruding jaw. "Ain't no way I'm going back home either, except maybe to visit my family. There's a lot of world out there, and I aim to see it." My head tingled as the barber made the first pass over my scalp, a reverse Mohawk dead center to the back of my neck. "Pickings won't be that good for you soon enough," he snickered.

It took the barber less than a minute to shave my head as close as a Buddhist novice monk's. "Man, will you look at this?" I whined at my reflection. "Why does the Army have to do this? We look like faces somebody drew on eggs."

"Maybe to keep down head lice," Jonathan snickered. I watched him grinning at the back of my head.

"Yeah, that's what the Army says, but it's gotta be more than that. You can always wash your hair."

His reflected grin slowly dissolved into a frown. "Turn us into something we ain't, I expect. Kind of like the way my people used to turn boys into men every spring."

"Yeah," I exclaimed in what I thought was a burst of understanding. "Like an initiation ceremony. I've read about how those rituals are meant to shuck off childhood, like a snake shedding old skin. Only in our case, it's shucking off civilian clothes and hair."

The barber finished and I stood and faced Jonathan. "Not exactly an initiation, but similar," he replied. "My grandfather says life is one initiation after another because every change means something old must die before anything new can be born."

Jonathan started outside and I followed. "Never thought I needed to die to childhood, or being a civilian, or anything else," I said as I jammed my field cap over my baldness. "Besides, what the hell will scalping make us into?"

"Like you said, 'soldiers,'" he laughed.

"Fall in! Now! Move your asses or I'll have them shaved too!" the drill sergeant screamed.

Recruit Company 1706 quickly unfolded into four relatively straight lines of twenty bewildered, hairless, egg-shaped heads. "Your grandfather sounds like a smart man," I whispered as the drill sergeant called us to attention. "Like to meet him sometime." The drill sergeant walked up to me, stopped, glared into my eyes, then passed to the head of the company. "At least we fit in here," I whispered.

"That'll be different," Jonathan said. "Never done that before. Might be a nice change."

It was during basic training that I found out what Jonathan Blue Heron wanted most was to be a white man more than a drunk wants a bottle of cheap whiskey. But I didn't know why until much later after I met his sister and grandfather. The plain fact was I tied up with an Indian Sisyphus pushing his private boulder up a mountain only to have it roll back just before he reached the top. Once it did, the only thing he could do was run like hell as it chased him to the bottom. He never learned and it never crossed his mind to back away. He just kept pushing that damned rock back up the mountain. And it always rolled back on him. To this day I don't understand how—or even why—we became friends.

Recruit training and combat have one thing in common: no one knows why anyone does anything. It's a life of intimacy without privacy or individuality, with hierarchy piled on hierarchy like Chinese puzzle boxes. Squad, company, regiment, division, brigade, corps, Army in ascending order with lives more valuable than the ones below. Nothing has less value than a single soldier. So, we become friends in self-defense. Jonathan and I were both loners, but for different reasons. We needed each other to keep from drowning in olive-green conformity. But it doesn't take long for new recruits to accept the Army's focus on rooting out all individuality. One of the first things you learn is that in combat individuality can get a man—or a division—killed. That's why men between the ages of eighteen and twenty-five make the best soldiers. They lack experience and want it like pigs want slop, are group-centered, and easy to convince. Where else can you find men willing to put trash cans on their heads and call themselves shitheads because the drill sergeant doesn't like the way they made their bunks or cleaned the latrine or reassembled an M-16? In only ten weeks any army in the world can indoctrinate a company of seventy-five young men fresh out of school into dividing the world into good and evil.

The Army makes life as simple as a John Wayne movie. Enemies are human beings the government decided for whatever reason are evil. Killing legally defined "enemies" is not murder, but justice, and a man's personal morality doesn't count. At the end of basic training, he will most likely believe four things: he is a man, he is a natural killer and very good at it, death in combat grants him moral stature above all civilians, and he will gladly die for his country. Men over twenty-five know better. They have experience and are skeptical. A graduate from basic training's first firefight is enough to turn him into a skeptic, but by then it's too late, and there's only one thing to do: fight and die, and in between learn the hard lesson—that strings of events happen in interlocking sequences and find their own order that's not necessarily chronological. Time becomes myth and events *are* time, not *in* time, a continuous web of revelation for those having eyes to see and ears to ear.

My tour in Vietnam revealed how some men loved war. War gives them a hard-on and makes them feel alive, something they never felt in the humdrum of civilian life. They lose their interest in school, marriage, family, and going to work every day. So, when war rips them from normalcy, life becomes the bait and killing the hook. Desire and fear, the two emotions that govern all living things, suddenly seemed watered down by peacetime like good whisky in a cheap saloon. War makes them suffer, but by God, they are alive.

After basic and before we arrived in Vietnam, Jonathan's war was local and private. His enemy was himself and the Haida people, and his primary weapon was alcohol. Vietnam expanded his war and gave him life as he never knew it the moment we landed at Tan Son Nhut Air Base in a charted United Airlines DC-8, where we hooked up with a redneck kid from Arkansas named Billy Joe Johnson. We marched past a stack of aluminum coffins and live human beings waiting to board a C-141 for the States and herded into a dark hanger with a sign painted in red letters and faded gold that read, "Welcome to Vietnam, Republic Of," and full doctors and nurses giving shots and filling out paperwork and officers giving orders and assigning transport to field units. After eight hours of hurry-up-and-wait followed by a four-hour ride in a deuce and a half that was part of a supply convoy headed for Nha Trang, we were dropped off at An Loc at dusk, where we were met by a staff sergeant named Adams, who ordered us to get the hell off the truck and into his jeep. He drove us to a bunker in a clearing on the east side of Firebase Alice manned by Third Platoon, Delta Company, First Cavalry Division, two hundred meters from the jungle.

"Time to get you cherries settled in," Adams grumbled as we pulled up to a rectangular sandbagged bunker rigged over a hole. "This is your hootch, provided it don't get overrun by them dink bastards waiting in the bush for your young asses."

We strained to catch a glimpse of who might be watching us through the darkening twilight behind the tree line. "How close?" I remember asking.

"Close enough," Adams answered nervously. "Last CO we had shacked up with a dink, only he didn't know it. So, one night they're in the sack and she slits his throat and cuts off his balls with a razor. He was found in the morning with his testicles stuffed in his mouth."

"Sweet Jesus," Billy Joe gasped. "What did they tell his folks?"

"Killed in action, shit-for-brains," Adams snarled. "He was an officer. What do you think they'd say?"

Jonathan exploded with laughter.

"Shut the fuck up," Adams snarled. "No one said you could laugh." He jumped in front of Jonathan and tried to stare him down. Jonathan stood calmly, his arms hanging limp at his sides. That's when Jonathan's troubles with Adams started. He didn't back down from Adams—then or after. The small mocking smile that folded Jonathan's mouth into a tight crescent really set Adams off. Jonathan never blinked as he returned Adam's stare with a vacant look of his own. He did this every time he saw or spoke to Adams.

Adams finally yelled, "You got no right to laugh," as he turned and headed into the hootch.

We stumbled after him down a ramp carved in red clay four feet into a barely lit fifteen-by-ten pit. Triple rows of sandbags rose three feet above the ground on all sides. Heavy timbers reinforced with more sandbags covered the hootch with a flat roof. The only openings were gun slits on the four walls and the entrance. Eight pairs of eyes blankly focused on us through dark, stale air cloudy with sweat and mildew.

"What the hell we got here?" crooned a tall, black first sergeant with the letters HNIT stenciled in black letters over the left pocket of his fatigue shirt.

"Fresh meat," Adams answered. He read out names from our orders. "This here is Elwin, Johnson, and . . . Blue Heron?" He looked up at Jonathan. "What the hell kind of name is that?"

"Indian," Jonathan hissed as he dropped his gear on the dirt floor.

"Speak up, boy," Adams barked.

"You heard me," Jonathan growled.

"Well, I'll be damned," Adams mocked. "What we've got here is an Injun. A natural-born scout. As of now, you're permanent point man, boy." Then he pointed at Billy Joe and me. "Don't know about these two."

"We'll break 'em in right," the first sergeant said.

Adams headed out the door. "Starting in the morning, you and Third Squad."

"Thought we were supposed to get orientation," Billy Joe drawled.

"You will, Sweet Cheeks," Adams answered. "In the goddamn bush. The VC are the best instructors there are."

"We're still short," the first sergeant called after Adams.

"You'll have to make do."

After Adams left, the veterans of Second Squad silently looked us over. That's when I came to know one of war's facts of life. We were new to the squad whose rookie mistakes could get a veteran killed. Which meant our deaths were unimportant. But an old-timer's death was a moral outrage, and we were expendable. Any rookie who survived long enough to become an old-timer didn't deserve getting killed because a new replacement didn't know anything. The first sergeant broke the silence. "Don't pay Adams no attention. Son of a bitch is crazy as hell. But he knows what's up in a fight. Stow your gear and find an empty cot."

Second Squad's expressionless eyes continued giving us the once-over as we settled in. "Might as well do the honors," the first sergeant said. He thumbed his right hand to a short thickset kid with red hair cropped short. "This here's Kelly. He's an Irish honky but treat him with respect anyway. He's our medic. Never let anything happen to Kelly."

"Drink to that," Kelly replied.

"Shit, Kelly, you'll drink or smoke to anything," a tall man standing by the door said.

"That black brother there," the first sergeant said, "is Washburn. Best for you not to make any mistakes in the boonies tomorrow. He's apt to kill you."

"Got that right," Washburn said. "Going back to the world in three weeks. Ain't nothing going to stop this boy from going home and giving every round eye he can some prime Louisiana black snake."

"That there's Mayburn, Stokes, Prager, Washington, and Tolson. I'm Albert Jackson. I'm the HNIT in this squad."

"What's that mean?" Billy Joe asked.

"Boy, you from the South, ain't ya?"

"Arkansas," Billy Joe answered. "So?"

"So, this will really piss you off. I'm the head negro in town. Got to be that in the meanest part of Philadelphia 'cause I fight like a junkyard dog. To you, boy, that means squad leader. And don't any of you go calling me 'Sarge.' Albert is good enough."

"Tell me about Adams," Jonathan interrupted. "The bastard and I are gonna tangle."

"Man, slow down!" Albert said abruptly. "Don't nobody mess with Adams."

"He gets his rocks off killing people." Mayburn said. "Don't matter to him which side they're on."

Albert sat on his cot and looked around the hootch. "Guess it's up to me."

"You are the HNIT," Kelly snickered.

Daniel's expression got suddenly serious. "Going out at night, medics sometimes give you pills. Never take them myself. But Adams did two tours before doing long-range recon for the Forth Division. He popped pills like candy. He still does."

"Adams was a lurp?" I blurted. "I've heard stories about lurps."

"Most are true," Albert said. "Adams took pills by the fistful whenever he went out on a night ambush, which was all he ever did. Uppers to cut trail and downers to send him back."

"Crazy bastard told me they cooled things down for him," Stokes said. "He claimed they helped him see through the jungle at night. Like he was looking through a telescope."

Albert nodded. "He told me that too. During his first tour, he was the only survivor in a platoon of Cav wiped out going into La Drang Valley. He joined up with Special Forces during his second tour. Walked into an ambush then. He hid under the bodies of his team while the VC walked around with knives making sure. Stripped most of the bodies, they did, and walked away laughing. After that, there wasn't anything left for him but the lurps."

"What's a lurp?" I asked.

"Short for long-range reconnaissance patrol," Albert said.

"He really stepped in the shit that time," Prager whispered.

"Wasn't the last time," Tolson added.

Albert leaned back against a wall. "After that, they sent him back to the world, but he couldn't hack it. Told me after he got home, he just sat in his room all day. Sometimes he stuck a rifle out the window, leading people and cars as they passed his house. Got to the point that the only thing he could feel was the tip of his trigger finger. It really put his folks up tight."

"Christ, he puts people here up tight," Kelly whispered.

Mayburn shuttered. "I'm sorry, man. He's just too crazy for me. Just look at his eyes. The whole story's right there."

"Yeah, but better do it quick," Kelly said. "If he catches you at it . . ."

"He always seems to watch for it," Tolson interrupted. "All I ever managed was one quick look." He slowly shook his head. "I never saw anything that empty."

"Tits on a bull, man," Albert said. "The sarge is in the last six months of his tour. We got him because he's too damned mean for the lurps."

Billy Joe shifted nervously. "What happened?"

Albert took a cigarette from behind his ear and lit up. "What I heard," he said as he exhaled, "is that he went out with a patrol about ten clicks northwest of here. He came back alone. So, he paints himself up like a bad dream for night stalking, goes out alone, and comes back the next morning with a blindfolded prisoner with his elbows tied behind his back. The interrogation went on for two days straight. So did the screaming."

"So, they kick him out of the lurps and gave him to us?" Jonathan asked.

Albert glared at Jonathan. "You ain't one of us. You got to earn that." He paused and watched a rat scamper across the dirt floor. "Don't be messing with the sarge. He can't be killed, but you sure as hell can.

"Cut the crap and get some sleep," Albert ordered. "Charlie's got his shit together this time, and we got to get back to the war early."

4

As morning sunlight poured through my pickup's windows, I woke to dull pain radiating in a band from my eyes to the center of my forehead to the top of my skull down the back of my neck. Emotions revolved inside the pain like a wheel within a wheel, and when I opened my eyes, my pickup like a third wheel revolved around the pain. Then I remembered where I was.

I was pulled in under a grove of fir trees in a small rest area on the Fraser River surrounded by low arid hills. Doppler whines from eighteen-wheelers passing on the highway in both directions intermingled with a flock of squawking crows roosting over my head in the trees. The river was fifty yards west, and I climbed out of the pickup and headed in that direction.

I wasn't hungover but took a drunk's cure anyway and jumped into a shallow pool just as I remembered that I was still dressed. The shock of the snow fed current hit me like a punch in the stomach and sucked the breath from my lungs. I sat on a rock in the current feeling stupid. When my head cleared, I walked back to the truck and put on dry clothes. I finished the cure with a cold breakfast of dry fruit and crackers, washed down by two cups of black coffee brought to a boil on a Colman stove. By 7:00 a.m. I was back on the road full of recollections in need of focus. Sure as hell, the world has signed a pact with the devil. Everything's bound to it and the terms are clear. If you want to live you have to die. How did Born of Songs put it? You can't have mountains and creeks without space, and space is a beautiful woman married to a blind man. The blind man is Time, and he doesn't go anywhere without his great dog, Death. Physics calls it the second law of thermodynamics.

The space-time I moved through was semiarid country painted acrylic gold by the morning sun. Low mountain and river canyon country open to the sky and dotted with farms and wooded sections cultivated with no secrets. But the land began a metamorphosis an hour up Route 97, where the Thompson River runs into the Fraser River near Lytton. Sounds become more defined, sights sharper, and touch more sensitive. Feelings and reactions I learned in combat, but repressed by five years of civilian life, gradually returned like lost friends. Jonathan was sober, and I would need these friends.

There wasn't much in Lytton except a gas station. It was one thirty in the afternoon when I stopped there for gas and polished off the last of the coffee in my thermos. Prince George was still seven hours away, so I figured I'd push on until late afternoon, haul in somewhere before dark, then drive straight through in the morning to Prince Rupert and call Jamie. She could decide the next move. From Lytton the two-lane winds through three river valleys: the Fraser, Thompson, and Quesnel. It's heavily forested country whose people earn their living by logging, farming, fishing, and hunting. The number of settlers surprised me. Mostly in small towns and settlements hugging Route 97 like beads on a rosary. Beyond the mountains surrounding both sides of the highway a few trappers, Indians, and white loners live with forces hidden deep within wilderness far from civilized eyes. I had no idea how strong these forces were until that night six years ago when Nathan Born of Songs whispered that life is a crooked path between opposite powers rising like mountains to the Sky Father.

It happened after graduation from Army basic training. It takes ten weeks for the Army to turn recruits and draftees into soldiers. Those who make it are rewarded with a two-week furlough. I had no place to go, no family to see. My mother, father, and older brother were killed by a drunk driving a pickup just before I turned seventeen. Lawsuits and life insurance provided enough money for college, so I mostly lived at Stanford University or wherever I found summer work until graduation. I had relatives scattered in the Midwest, but I didn't know them and didn't feel inclined to. So I went home with Jonathan, up the Unuk River north of Ketchikan near Misty Fjords National Monument on the US side of the Alaska-Canadian border.

It's always wet there. November is the wettest month. Days are short, nights long, with drenching rains keeping the land as misted and muted as the design of winter night painted on a Japanese scroll. Nathan Born of Songs lived in deliberate simplicity in this wet isolation in a rundown two-room log cabin on five acres of cleared land surrounded by old-growth Sitka spruce and red cedar. The only way to get there was a narrow dirt road snaking from the main highway up the Unuk River that dead-ended at the cabin. The only safe way to get there is by a four-wheel drive car or truck. So, except for Jonathan and Jamie, Born of Songs had few visitors. His isolation was as complete as possible for a man living in the twentieth century.

But while Born of Songs may have lived in nearly complete isolation, he was never alone. He shared the land with a large population of grizzly bears, and he claimed it was with their permission. Maybe so. The land crawled with grizz and with flocks of ravens always roosting near his cabin. "They're family," he once told me. "You're never alone with your family," as he howled in laughter at the mystified expression that crossed my face.

Jonathan often spoke of his grandfather during basic training—to me and no one else. That in itself was strange. What was even stranger was the mix of respect and anger in his words. I only learned two things about Born of Songs before I met him: he lived isolated in the mountains, and he was a Haida shaman. Everything Jonathan said about his grandfather was beyond my experience. Which meant I didn't know what to expect the first time I laid eyes on him. But I was curious as hell.

He didn't seem like much at first. Just a dried-up old man with the rubbed features and the stooped shoulders of a postal clerk. He wasn't very imposing. Except for his eyes. They were jet black, but they never seem to stay that way. Born of Songs could change their color according to his mood: fire orange when he was angry, green when he concentrated on something, and sort of brown when he was content. There were times when his eyes flashed through these colors like a blinking neon. I still don't know how he did it.

There was something else about him. Born of Songs always wore the same red plaid hunting shirt with Levies bleached gray with age and stuffed into calf-length seal hide moccasins. Leastwise, I never saw him dressed any other way. He tied his shoulder-length hair off his forehead with an elk hide bandana so tight that it seemed to pull his eyes wider apart than normal above a large, hooked nose that stuck out from his oval face like an arrowhead. We didn't talk much for the first week and a half. He didn't ignore me. He just studied me. It was rather unnerving as I tried to ignore him, mostly because I was more interested in Jamie Bear Mother's Daughter.

She didn't say much either. She just watched her brother and me as intently as Born of Songs through eyes as black as patent leather buttons floating in a saucer of milk. The fact is, she made me uneasy too. She had a sensual presence I wanted to touch but was afraid to because I didn't know how. So, I just watched and kept my distance. When we did talk, it was mostly about nothing I was interested in. Polite, small talk didn't seem to interest her either. What was Army life like? When was I going to Vietnam? Would I be stationed with Jonathan? Did I have a family? What were my plans after the war?

After three days Jonathan got bored as hell. When I suggested we head out for Seattle, he said it was too much of a hassle. So, he slept most of the time, and when he wasn't sleeping, he just sat around the cabin staring at nothing in particular as he drank whisky from a bottle he always carried with him. His energy just disappeared, as if the land itself had sucked him dry. But it was all right with me. The country surrounding the cabin was beautiful and it was good to kick back from the Army and from thinking about Vietnam. So, I slept late, took quiet walks in the forest with Jamie, talked small talk, and relaxed into the solitude.

Then on a rainy night two days before we had to leave, Born of Songs said something that still burns into my memory like a low-grade fever. He paused and listened to the rain pounding hard on the cabin's shake roof, and said, "Most of the time, a man walks his path alone."

We were sitting in a semicircle around the fireplace. Born of Songs was leaning back on a bear skin spread over a homemade cedar chair with his stubby legs stretched out toward the fireplace. I was slumped on an ancient couch covered by a Navajo blanket, more interested in watching Jamie than in anything Born of Songs had to say. She sat beside me, her eyes locked into mine, like a hunter reading animal signs. "Women too," I mumbled with a touch of sarcasm.

Born of Songs leaned forward and clasped his hands over his knees. "Especially women," he whispered. "A man's life dies and is made again, by women."

"What's that mean?" I glanced at Born of Song, then tried to read Jamie's expression for clues.

"Not a damn thing," Jonathan cued in harshly. He was straddled over a folding chair with his arms hanging limply across the back.

Born of Songs glared at him, then softened his gaze. "It means that woman is within hard things. Stones, minerals, earth, wood, and soft things like water. She is permanent. She controls and creates. She owns breath and air and wind. Men come and go, but woman is what continues because she is what stays."

"This is your culture, man," I said to Jonathan. "What's he talking about?" Jonathan shrugged his shoulders, scowled, and took a drink of Jack Daniels.

"Sorry, sir," I said to Born of Songs. "I don't follow. I thought you were referring to some kind of road."

"I still am," Born of Songs laughed as he winked at Jamie. "Sometimes good spirits ambush a man on his road. Sometimes bad spirits. It's not easy to tell which. But sometimes friends from two different worlds walk the same path." Jamie moved to the fireplace and tossed in a piece of alder. She watched the fire build, then sat back on the couch, and refocused her eyes on me. "When that happens, one friend's helpers become the other friend's demons, and one friend's demons become the other friend's helpers."

My attention was focused on Jamie, but Born of Song's words began to pull me away. "I still don't understand," I said softly.

Born of Songs exhaled in exasperation. "Friends become enemies and enemies become friends."

Jonathan pounded his bottle of Jack Daniels on the floor. "I don't understand him either," he slurred.

"Better take it easy on that stuff," Jamie said. She stood and walked to the cook stove opposite the fireplace and poured coffee from an iron pot into a large white mug. "Looks like you'll both learn the hard way," she continued. She brought the cup to Born of Songs, then returned to her place next to me.

"I'm not the one who needs this," Born of Songs muttered. He lifted the mug to his lips with thick hands calloused from hard work. "When I was young," he said as he lowered the cup, "I thought I knew it all too."

"I meant no disrespect," I said. "Neither did Jonathan."

"None taken," Born of Songs whispered.

"Leave it alone," Jonathan blustered. He kicked the empty Jack Daniels bottle across the floor. "Just an old man's nightmare. It's got nothing to do with anything."

"Knock it off, man," I whispered to Jonathan. Jonathan glared at me through the bloodshot eyes of a drunk. "Please, I want to understand," I said to Born of Songs. "I don't know why, but—"

Jonathan jumped to his feet and stumbled toward the bedroom. "Got no time for this crap. All you want to do, you bastard, is ball my sister."

"You son of a bitch," I blurted after him as he drew the dirty gray curtain that separated the small bedroom from the rest of the cabin. The trail of tension and anger he left behind could have been cut with a knife. "I'm sorry," I muttered. "I don't know what brought that on."

"The fault is not yours," Born of Songs said gently. "My grandson's tired of being what he is. He wants to be like you."

"Like me? What do you mean?"

"He wants to be a white man."

"He what?"

"He wants to be a white man," Born of Songs repeated.

Jonathan's boots hit the bedroom floor with a thud and the bed springs squeaked with the strain of is body as he plopped hard on the mattress.

"I don't understand," I said. "There's nothing wrong with being an Indian." I glanced at Jamie. "Fact is, it's a good thing. Why would he want to be a white man?"

"He thinks our ways are dead," Born of Songs answered. "He believes the world has turned white and our people don't belong anymore. He thinks the only way he can live in a white world is to be a white man."

"But why? How can he change what he is? That's a dead end."

"That's true as far as it goes," Jamie said. "The only thing I can think of is some bad spirit is taking over his mind. He is convinced that the Haida Way keeps my people oppressed. You know the story. Our men are always drunk. They don't go to school and can't get work even when they do. And our women stay home making babies to add to welfare rolls. He believes all the white stereotypes about my people are true."

"There's got to be more to it than that," I said. "Something really bad must have happened to him."

"It wasn't any one thing, but lots of things," Jamie continued. "Seems like he never fit in with my people since the day he was born. Things always went bad for him, so nothing ever worked out. It came to a head when he got a job on a fishing boat just before he was drafted by the Army."

"What happened?" I asked.

Jamie looked away and hesitated. "It's a long story. I'll tell you later."

"He often told me he didn't like being Indian, but I just thought he was scared about going to Vietnam.

"It's not Vietnam," she said. "The truth is he's looking forward to it."

"That's not the only truth," Born of Songs added. "My grandson is like a coyote that wants to be a wolf. Both will kill him if he tries." He stood and spread the bearskin over his shoulders.

"I think I see . . ."

"You see nothing," he whispered, "because you are too much like my grandson to see what's going on here."

"Jonathan's my best friend," I protested. "He's not as dumb as you think, and neither am I. We'll get each other through this war."

Born of Songs stood and folded his arms across his chest. His eyes flashed indigo as he stared into my eyes. "You're white," he said softly. "You've bumped into my grandson's life"—he nodded to Jamie—"maybe our lives like a tourist. Take pictures, buy trinkets, go home so you can tell your friends you're an expert on Indians."

"No way that's true," I objected.

"Grandfather meant no insult," Jamie whispered. "This is the way white people usually deal with my people. He's only worried about you and my brother. There will be hard times when you and Jonathan leave the circle of power in these mountains."

"Circle of power? I have no idea what that means. All I know is that we'll have each other's backs and try to come home alive."

Born of Songs exhaled slowly as his eyes darkened to black. "Your war only begins in Vietnam. It will not end there, but here."

Before I could reply, Born of Songs nodded to Jamie as he stood and walked towards the cabin door. "I'll be at Raven's House," he said in a voice as mournful as a man attending a funeral."

As Born of Songs started to leave, I put my right hand on his shoulder and said, "Please tell me what's going on."

As he turned the color of his eyes glowed red. "You really want to know? Better be careful," he warned. "Some knowledge isn't free."

I tried to turn away but couldn't move. "What knowledge?" I gasped.

"Innocence," he said flatly. He turned and spoke to Jamie as he stepped out the door. "If you think this white man is worthy, bring him to Raven's House in the morning."

Jamie didn't answer. We stood in silence and watched Born of Songs disappear into the darkness. "Where's he going?" I finally asked.

She shut the door and latched it. "Grandfather built a traditional Haida house many years ago on top of a small mountain about three miles from here." She went to a closet and pulled three wool blankets from the top shelf. "He calls it Koyah's House. In our language, it means, 'Raven's House.' He spends lots of time there. More time than ever since Jonathan joined the Army. I used to spend lots of time there myself before I started teaching at the Indian school in Ketchikan." She turned and smiled. "He honors you by asking me to bring you there."

"It's awfully cold and dark out there. I hope he doesn't get lost."

She softly laughed as she began to spread the blankets on the floor in front of the fireplace. "He won't," she whispered with quiet certainty.

"I feel like a witness to a wreck watching someone bleed to death because I don't know what to do," I said.

She looked up and smiled. "That's because you don't know what you've stepped into."

A gust of wind slammed rain hard against the cabin and pushed large drops down the chimney. The sound of sizzling coals blended into the sound of Jonathan's snoring filtering in from the bedroom. "What don't I know about your brother?" I asked.

Jamie folded her legs under her as she sat on the blankets. "Why are you standing?" She pointed to a spot on the blanket next to her. "Come, sit here."

"What don't I know about Jonathan?" I repeated as I sat and crossed my legs.

"You know the symptoms. He drinks too much, he hates being Haida, wishes he wasn't. But you don't understand the disease."

"Maybe not, but I'm not particularly happy about my people either, so maybe I can understand Jonathan's problems. At least partially. The more we know about each other, the better our chances for coming home from Vietnam alive."

She folded her hands on her lap and listened briefly to Jonathan's breathing. "All right," she began. "Here it is. About four years ago Jonathan was a hand on a deep-sea fishing boat that worked the Gulf. The boats are out for weeks at a time in constant rough water."

"I've heard it's hard and dangerous work," I said. "Lots of men die every year, mostly by drowning."

She nodded. "Jonathan was glad to get signed on. He hadn't worked for over a year, and times being what they were, there wasn't much work for Haida men. We lived here with Grandfather then, but Jonathan wanted to be on his own. That takes money, which we didn't have. So, he jumped at the chance to get away when a white boat owner agreed to take him on."

"It sounds like he got a break. But you said he didn't have skills. What did he know about fishing boats?"

"Nothing," she answered. "But my people have fished in these waters for hundreds of years."

"So, crewing on a white man's fishing boat was the only job that opened up for Jonathan?" I asked.

She gazed at her folded hands. "That and logging. He saw it as a way out."

"A way out of what?"

"Being poor. Being dependent on Grandfather, getting out of these mountains, a way out of everything he thinks keeps him down."

"He took the job, and it didn't work out," I guessed. "Something bad must have happened.

"It was good at first. The owner—his name was Stark—treated him well. He gave Jonathan the easiest jobs and always bragged about how fast he learned. Jonathan didn't even have to stand watches. And Stark promised him a larger share of the catch than the rest of the crew. Six weeks out, Stark got to drinking and talking too much, and the crew found out."

"And they weren't happy," I said.

"It came near to mutiny. At least as Jonathan tells it, they were going to kill him. They were poor white men, poorer than Jonathan. Most of them had families, and none of them were making it. There was no way they'd let a Haida man get special treatment. Anyway, Stark tried to convince them that Jonathan deserved the extra 'bonus,' as he called it."

"Guess that didn't set well. Stark sounds like a fool."

"A scared fool," Jamie said. "The most dangerous kind. They were a long way out, and like you said, lots of fishermen drown in the Gulf of Alaska every fishing season. It would have been easy to make Jonathan and Stark disappear. So, Stark reneged on the deal."

"So, Jonathan got an equal share with the crew?" I asked. "It depends on the seize of the catch, but that doesn't sound bad. That's what Stark should have offered in the first place."

"That's what should have happened, but it didn't. After they filled the boat's hold with salmon and returned to Ketchikan, Jonathan got nothing."

"Nothing?"

"Not a cent," Jamie answered.

"They ripped him off," I said. "Didn't he do anything about it?"

"He tried, "but Stark's boat was a Gypsy operation."

"What's that mean?"

"He wasn't part of the Fishermen's Union. He owned the boat and only signed on non-union crew. He paid them what he wanted and kept most of the profit himself. The fact is, he never intended to pay Jonathan anything."

"That's exploitation pure and simple," I said angrily. "There are laws against that."

Jamie took my hand and squeezed hard. "I love your passion for justice," she laughed." The trouble is that justice is white around here. Jonathan complained, all right. To Fish and Wildlife, to the police, to the Haida Tribal Council. They all said get a lawyer and take the bastard to court."

"Did he?" I asked.

"That costs money, which Jonathan didn't have," she answered. "Lawyers won't take cases unless lots of money is paid up-front, or if they become famous because it sets a new president. So, my brother gave up in disgust and joined the Army."

"Because he saw a chance to get out," I guessed. "I knew he didn't like it here. He told me that much. In fact, when I first met him, all he talked about was getting away from Ketchikan."

"And from Grandfather and me." A deep sadness welled up in Jamie's eyes.

"But I never knew why," I said. "Just that something was eating at him."

"Now you understand," she said in a voice I could hardly hear.

"At least better than I did," I said as I took her hands into mine. "But it makes me mad as hell. No one should be treated that way. Just because he's Haida. It's . . ."

Jamie pulled her hands away. "Like white people want us to apologize for the way the Creator made us," she interrupted. "So, who does Jonathan bring home on his first furlough? A white man he says is his friend."

"We're friends, all right," I said. "Just seems natural. I never thought about why. I didn't need to, I guess."

"You're the first white man I've met who didn't tie strings to friendship," Jamie replied as she fixed her eyes on mine.

I felt my face flush. I didn't know what to say. I could only watch as she leaned to one side and begin to spread the blankets into a bed in front of the fireplace. When she finished, she looked at me, smiled broadly, and said, "Stay with me tonight. I don't want to be alone. Neither do you."

I felt what all twenty-year-old men feel who live mostly with the flat angularities of other young men. All women seem round and soft, all are inscrutable and fascinating. When an invitation is given, young men tend to freeze in uncertainty. For two weeks Jonathan and I slept in the same room with Jamie and Born of Songs in front of the fireplace. But now the invitation was given, and I knew what to do but not how to do it. So, I blurted in a fit of Presbyterian hesitation, "What about Jonathan?"

Her eyes seemed to dance with anticipation. "Jonathan will be unconscious until noon. You know he can't hold his liquor." She looked away at the coals hissing with drops of rain that fell through the chimney. "Besides," she said softly, "you've wanted me since you arrived."

I moved to her with eager clumsiness. "That's the truth," I said hoarsely.

We slowly undressed each other, like children taking wrappings of presents. Her brown skin was gilded bronze by the dimming firelight, and it pulled my breath away in deep gulps. As I tentatively touched her, it felt like I was stroking a wild and free spirit—a shock of delight that tied me to her rhythms. I merged and shook with them in a pleasure so intense it bordered on pain. At her apex she breathed, "Come inside me . . . now."

I did, and when I did, I found revelation. Nothing I had done before felt so self-evidently right. I felt aligned with powerful forces that in some curious way confirmed my existence. I lingered inside her, held her energy as she drew on mine, empowered by her femininity, until I could no longer hold back. And at that moment, everything changed. She took me to another level of reality. I wasn't going anywhere. I was completely here, in that space and time, fully and completely in the present. I wasn't waiting for anything to happen. It was happening, a fantastic lucky accident, a cosmic windfall.

Later that night, another truth came: I knew absolutely nothing about this woman except her name.

5

I drove north into a storm that flowed in a low line from the western range southeast to the Fraser River north of Cache Creek, half focused on the present, half on the past, trying to figure out the future. I felt like a man waking up from surgery, cut up, put back together, and lethargic. Sheets of hard rain peppered the windshield like BBs. I checked my speed and eased down from seventy to fifty. A southbound logging truck shot past on the shoulderless road, screaming air horn obscenities as it started up a small grade. The log truck's turbulence sucked my pickup left over the yellow dividing line toward a drainage ditch, and I instinctively eased up on the gas and corrected back on track.

It was definitely time to pull off the road. I did, under a grove of hemlocks and opened the left side window. A mixture of cold rain and hail pelted my face as I gulped the air's freshness. When I was able to relax, I rolled up the window, leaned back, and shut my eyes, my memories locked into recollections of war mixed with anticipation of what waited for me up the road. It was a curious dream chemistry, like being a catalyst for something about to happen. But what? The closer I got to Ketchikan, the more the past pulled itself into my memory and seemed more real than the present. Some memories, the most powerful ones, come unbidden like Chinese hungry ghosts and fuse dreams with reality.

The dream was of a day and a song. A soft chant wrapped in Jamie's voice that morning as we prepared to go to Raven's house. She was standing by the woodstove cooking breakfast. Fresh coffee perked beside sizzling bacon and eggs, and the sounds and smells nurtured her song the way a jazz combo backgrounds its lead singer. I didn't understand the language, but when she heard me shift in the blankets she jumped into English.

I have taken a woman of beauty for my wife,
I have taken her from her friends.
I hope her kinsmen will not come,
    and take her away from me.
I will be kind to her.
Berries, berries I will give her from
    the hill,
And roots from the ground.
For her I made this song and for her
    I will sing it.

I didn't understand the meaning any better in English. But it was still beautiful. Hell, she could have done or said almost anything, and I would have thought it was as beautiful as the long black hair that spread over her shoulders down to her waist like an inverted fan. When I asked her about the song, she turned and looked at me with an easy and relaxed expression, with no evidence of the strain I felt flowing from her body during the night.

"Just something Grandfather taught me when I was a little girl," she answered. "I always sing it when I'm happy." She reached for the coffee, poured a cup, and brought it to me. "Grandfather says anyone who sings this song is a friend of the Bear People."

It was pure truth. I couldn't remember when I was so flat-out content and in harmony with everything around me. I wrapped a blanket around my shoulders and looked out the window. The landscape looked like a watercolor, and I took it all in as I sipped my coffee. A silver mist hung over the forest like a bleached animal hide, here and there streaked with narrow shafts of sunlight the color of liquid butterscotch that poured from blue breaks in the winter gray sky.

"Are you hungry?" Jamie asked as she dished our breakfast on metal plates—scrambled eggs, bacon, fresh biscuits, butter, and wild blackberry jam.

I don't know if it was love or lust or a combination, but I was as voracious as a pack of hungry wolves at entrails. "I'm starved," I replied.

"Hungry white men are dangerous," she teased.

"A good thing to remember," I teased back.

"Sit by the fire," she said. "I'll bring it to you."

I tossed more wood into the fire and made a place beside me for her to sit. "What about Jonathan?" I asked as I shoved a biscuit smothered in blackberry jam and butter into my mouth.

"You asked that question last night," she teased.

I felt my face redden. "Guess I did."

She smiled. "He'll be out for hours." She glanced at the bedroom and listened. "Can't even hear him breathe," she said as she took a sip of coffee. "I love my brother, but damn it he's his own worst enemy."

"You hate what he's done to himself," I said.

"Is doing to himself," she corrected.

I stopped eating and watched her. She wanted something and was being cagey.

"Jonathan loves you like a brother," she continued. "He has no brothers and has always wanted one."

"We're friends. It's that simple."

She nodded her head. "Yes, but it's not simple."

"Sure enough it's become that way," I said. "Especially now."

She sat her coffee down and folded her hands on her lap. "You think the world is the only one you see with your eyes and hear with your ears and touch with your hands," she said with soft intensity. "My people know many worlds, all full of spirits and animal ancestors that give life and death and everything in between." She paused and took a deep breath. "Spirits and animal ancestors exist in your world too. When they appear, you call them 'hallucinations' and go see a psychiatrist."

"When your people see them, you go see a shaman," I said. "So what?"

"So, plenty. My people know they're real. They're family. We go crazy when we separate ourselves from their power. Your people separate yourselves from your ancestors—and your past—and are always crazy."

"I can't argue with that," I said. "But right now, I've got enough to worry about. In about ten days, your brother and I will be covering each other's butts for twelve months in a very dangerous place. I need to know if I can rely on him, and I need to know what's going on between us."

"Are you sure that's what you want?"

"Damn it," I blurted. "How many times do I have to say it?"

Jamie didn't answer right away as she gathered the breakfast dishes and carried them to the kitchen sink. After a long, awkward silence she began speaking in a hushed tone. "Be careful. You will enter the empty spaces between your world and Jonathan's and mine. In that limbo, things will not be as you have ever known." She returned to the blankets and sat. "It will be dangerous for you and Jonathan and me."

"How's that?" I asked.

"To keep Jonathan's friendship and to keep what we have found, you must become one of us—a Haida man—and stay what you always will be—a white man. You must learn to live and think as you live in the overlap of these two worlds."

Young men full of hormones and juice are irrational and will promise anything to a woman they think they love. "Whatever that means," I snapped. "The main thing is, I won't back away."

"We'll see," she replied coolly. "Get dressed. It's time to go to Raven's House. Things have a way of becoming clearer there."

"I've wondered about that place since Born of Songs left last night."

"It's a traditional red cedar plank house. Grandfather built it many years ago on a cleared hill surrounded by the forest. Did you know that red cedar is sacred to my people?"

She took my hands and pulled me to my feet. I wrapped her in my arms and said, "No, I didn't," and brushed her lips with mine.

She pulled back and looked deeply into my eyes again and said, "You'll go there with me? Even knowing there are no guarantees?"

"Let's get started," I answered.

She pulled away and I watched her walk into the bedroom and draw the curtain after her. The first time I felt the power of the forest was with Jamie during the night. I had no words to wrap around what I experienced, and it stunned me to silence. Then, as I waited for Jamie, a word flashed like neon in my mind: "Life." Jamie and I ran together after life during the night. Then there came an opposite word that glowed with equal force: "Death." What I sensed was "Life" interdependent with "Death": two sides of the same coin. No one can hide from it. You can only live and die. The only question is, "How?" Looking back, that's why it was so easy for her to convince me to go to Raven's House. The old man was the source of this knowledge, and Jamie was the key that would unlock it for me.

Nor was I prepared for what I saw when Jamie came out of the bedroom. She was dressed in a cape woven of shredded, oiled cedar bark that hung midcalf from her shoulders over a plaid green hunting shirt. More shredded cedar bark woven into an apron with two rows of twined bark for a waistband was tied securely over her faded Levies stuffed into knee-high seal skin moccasins. Her hair was done up in long braids held in place by an undecorated buckskin headband. A single bear claw dangled across her breasts from a leather thong tied to her neck.

She hurried to the front door. "Ready?" she asked with a hint of impatience.

"Is that a special dress?" I asked as I put on my coat.

"It keeps the rain out. But I wear it mostly on special occasions, mostly ceremonies.

"We're going to a ceremony?"

She blinked and answered, "Maybe. That depends on Grandfather." She opened the door and stepped onto the porch. "Let's go before it starts raining again. I don't want to get wet."

"It's impossible not to get wet in this county," I complained. "What do you mean it depends on your grandfather?"

"On whether he thinks you are worthy to hear the story of my people." She exhaled her words as a breathy mist that disappeared into the humid air. "If Grandfather doesn't think you're ready, there will be no story and no ceremony. Then you'll be just another white tourist."

"That doesn't sound bad from where I'm standing," I teased.

She started across the clearing. "Yes," she said barely soft enough to hear. "It will be very sad."

I laughed under my breath as I buttoned my coat against the morning cold. "So, how will Born of Sons know when or if I'm ready?"

"How does a teacher know if any student is ready for knowledge? They just know. Grandfather's a shaman and he'll know."

She started walking faster once we entered the forest and I fell in behind. "Sounds simple enough," I quipped.

She suddenly wheeled around and her eyes, fierce as a sow bear defending cubs, stopped me dead in my tracks. "Born of Songs has power. You do not!" she snapped.

"Look, I apologize. Wish I knew for what, but I didn't mean to offend you or Born of Songs."

"Haida Ways must look crazy to white people," she muttered. She turned and started walking deeper into the forest. "Grandfather sees something in you. He thinks you are different from most white people. So do I."

There was no way I wasn't following her after that. I concentrated on her swaying hips and listened to the bottom of her cape brushing over tall clumps of wet bear grass. It was the only sound she made as we walked on a trail.

"The going gets hard," she whispered. "Pretty flat for starters, then a steep climb for two miles."

"Right behind you," I answered. "Don't worry about me."

After about twenty yards we lost sight of the cabin. Wispy fingers of mist sliced through the tops of red cedar and Sitka spruce and hung unmoving in the trapped humidity like wet spider webs. Shades of green darkened the forest floor into black decaying humus, broken only by remnants of tiny white flowers with half-unfolded petals, like the lips of people smiling at their own thoughts. The only sound was the slosh of our footsteps and the rain beginning to splash through the trees. After about a mile, the trail began to switch back sharply up a ridge and as we climbed sweat seeped through my shirt as if my body was trying to kick a fever.

"You're in good shape," I puffed.

"Don't talk," she ordered. "Didn't you see the signs?"

I scanned the brush and saw nothing except ground fog rising slowly over the trail. "What sign?" I asked.

"Grizz sign," she said. "Bear scat. We've passed several places where they've been feeding. Mostly sows with cubs."

It was time to get nervous and alert. The ground fog began to rise faster, like droplets of silver paint going against gravity.

"Haven't you seen the trees?" She pointed to several red cedars on both sides of the trail. "Look at the claw marks. You can see where they've rubbed their backsides. The grizz own this place. They're all around us." She tugged on my sleeve. "We've been spotted. Walk slow and pay attention. Your life depends on it."

"Not only my life. I've heard about grizzly sows with cubs." Movement in the bush caught my eye. "I wish like hell I had a gun."

"It's a good thing you don't. I can't let you kill family."

Fear began to flood my body. "Whatever the hell that means?" I focused on the movement in the brush as I tried to decide if we should run. "Something's up ahead, that's for sure."

"I see it. In that stand of ash up ahead. Stay put and don't move or say anything," she ordered firmly.

There wasn't anything else I could do. My legs seemed to lock as the possibility of movement slipped away from my body. Fear raced through my mind: It was a sow with cubs. There wasn't any place to run and we sure as hell couldn't outrun a pissed off sow grizz protecting her cubs. The wind kicked up and drove the rain harder. I looked around for the nearest tree. Sometimes you can escape a bear attack by climbing a tree.

Jamie pointed to a stand of thick ash. The movement stopped and she motioned me to stay put as she walked ahead in cadence with the song she sang as she prepared our breakfast. Her voice was low and husky, almost a growl. I stood transfixed on stiff legs that felt like spikes driven deep into the wet earth. The ground fog then condensed into a wet screen that blurred the outlines of trees into an aluminum haze. I could barely see Jamie. She stopped and waited as a massive shape charged out of the fog. Jamie slowly raised her arms and the fog lifted like a curtain to reveal a huge, snarling sow grizzly with twin cubs.

I tried running to Jamie to grab her and run, but the more I tried, the tighter fear squeezed my breath from my lungs. The sow reared up and snapped and roared her rage as it shook its massive head from side to side. Her front claws sliced the air like twin sets of five-inch knives. I tried to scream at her, but the sound stuck in my throat. Then Jamie lowered her arms and the sow dropped down to all fours and growled. The cubs scampered up to the sow, peeked curiously at me, then ran up to Jamie.

She knelt and scratched their ears and muzzles as she softly asked, "How are you, little brother and sister?"

The sow swayed from side to side. Her black tongue flicked back and forth over her snout as she picked up my scent. When Jamie stood up again, the cubs scampered back to the sow.

Jamie then spoke again. "Go in peace, Mother, as we do."

The sow snorted, turned, and ambled into the fog.

I finally managed to speak. "What the hell was that? Why aren't we dead?"

Jamie turned toward me and smiled. "There won't be any more trouble. We can go."

"Goddamn it, answer me!" I screamed. "What just happened?"

"Didn't you see?" she calmly answered. "We ran across a sow grizz with two cubs." She motioned to me. "Let's get moving. You're cold and wet. Raven's House is not far off."

She turned and started walking up the trail. I ran after her, pulled her to a stop, and spun her around by her shoulders. "I know what I saw but don't understand what I saw. That grizz could have killed us. Why didn't it?"

"Not us," she corrected. "She was going to kill you. That old grizz and her cubs are family."

"I need more than that," I demanded.

"Look," she tried to explain, "you're a white man. White people need permission to enter bear country. That old sow just gave her permission to you."

"Permission," I exclaimed.

"Pay attention, David. She was after you, not me. I'm a member of the Bear Clan."

It was my first lesson about Indian power. The only reason I was alive was because Jamie asked that sow grizz for my life. But it wasn't knowledge that brought me much comfort because it taught me the world wasn't what I thought it was. It wasn't the last lesson.

"Come, it's safe now," she gently coaxed as she started to walk.

By that time the fog had cleared, and I saw the trail snaking up a small treeless hill. Contrary impressions washed over me like the November rains that dampened the land. I shuffled forward, not so much by my own will, but more like being pulled by the confusing images that seemed to trail behind Jamie as we climbed: loving sister and granddaughter, passionate lover and protector of a confused white man, sorceress who spoke to a grizzly sow she called "Mother."

"What else is she?" I thought.

Jamie halted at the top of the hill. "We're here."

6

That last night on the road I parked under a grove of Sitka spruce fifty yards off the highway. Sleep was deep and without dreams until the silent shutdown of the forest noise brought me up alert the next morning. It was the kind of silence that warns prey of the presence of stalking predators. I heard it many times before in Vietnam, in the bush, when I was a predator hunting other human predators hunting me. I instinctively reached under the driver's seat for my Colt .45 and scanned the clearing surrounding my pickup. Then I knew what the silence was. The rain's monotone had stopped.

I opened the door and stepped into a wet chill that spasmed my neck and shoulder muscles into knots and settled into the iron rods that substituted for bones in my left shoulder, a memorial of a fight I shouldn't have survived, but did, because of Jonathan Blue Heron. Fog oozed over the mountains like gray gauze on the valley floor so thick that the air was liquid. Out of the fog a voice called from no particular direction, yet from all directions, no louder than a whisper, a grating sound like a parrot mimicking human speech. "Better hole up for a while," it said. "It's foolish to drive in fog this thick."

I heard this voice for the first time at Raven's House, but I hadn't heard it since that last nightmare in Vietnam. I never wanted to hear it again. But I wasn't afraid like before. Up the road I knew there were things waiting only an irrational man would not fear, real things, concrete things. After what I had been through in Vietnam, a disembodied bird voice was definitely no problem. "It's been a long time, Raven," I said out loud. I set up my two-burner Coleman and rummaged through my food box and found a jar of instant coffee and a bag of dried beef.

"You never know what you'll meet in fog," the voice cawed.

I pumped pressure into the Coleman. "I remember," I answered. After I turned on the burners and lit the hissing fuel, I opened a five-gallon water can and filled a small coffee pot and a larger aluminum pot and set them on the burners to boil.

"What do you remember?" the voice called. The question rolled out of the fog and wove around my skin like patterned wool.

"How I believed things were, what I know now, and the difference."

When the water in both pots began to boil, I wrapped a towel around my right hand, reached for the coffee pot, and set it on the food box. I dumped in a handful of instant coffee and let it set. Then I ripped open the dried beef bag and emptied it into the cooking pot. After about three minutes I turned off the gas, poured the coffee into a tin cup, and began eating out of the pot.

"It's good you remember," the voice said. "Life is more than what your eyes tell you. Physical eyes see only a mass of shapes. Some shapes are sharp and alive, others are not, and everything changes, fast or slow, tied to chains of cause and effect."

I took a swig of coffee. "Your words are too abstract, Raven," I answered, "like philosophy books. There's no life."

"The meaning's the same. White people believe things are separate. Have you forgotten?"

"I haven't forgotten. White logic teaches A is not B. Jonathan Blue Heron isn't me, animals can't be family, spirit helpers are superstition, and you can't be real."

"Now you know different."

I swallowed a mouthful of beef. "White logic is half-truth," I replied. "But everything is connected, like the threads of a spider's web."

The fog thickened the surrounding silence, and I knew I would not hear Raven's voice again until I returned to his house with Jamie. So, I dove deep into my mind as Nathan Born of Songs taught me to do when I needed to connect external events with internal meanings. "The time has finally come," I thought. "Either Jonathan will cure his madness, or he will die hard. The crazy son of a bitch had better come to his senses. Jamie and Jonathan Blue Heron want me to help him. But can you help a man who doesn't want help? Anything I do might get the three of us killed and rub out the Bear Clan. Damn it, I'm walking wide eyed into another ambush."

I finished eating, poured another cup of coffee, dumped the rest on the ground, and stowed the pot with my gear as I thought, "That damned fool doesn't want to be Haida, which means he's unable not to be Haida. So, he follows his path and drags us along with him, a drunk who's a maniac when sober, out of control, isolated, with no point to his life."

I cleared a spot in the rear of the pickup, climbed in, slammed the tailgate shut, took off my boots, unrolled a sleeping bag, and crawled in. "Who the hell am I in all this?' I whispered to myself. "Just another whacked off vet. Help Jonathan? Christ, who's going to help me, a white man acting like an Indian. Sweet Jesus, get real. If Jonathan's crazy, what the hell's that make me?"

I gulped down the rest of my coffee and leaned back and watched fog condense on the pickup's windows. Images of Raven's House flowed into my mind through visions projected on the pickup's windows, now like blackish gray video screens in the fading light, and flashed my mind back to the trail to Raven's House where Jamie and I finally broke through the fog at the top of a clear-cut hill bathed in sunlight. Four totem poles carved from huge red cedar logs rose into a topaz blue sky, as if stretched upward by invisible wires. One pole, the shortest, stood flush against the entrance of a rectangular cedar house covered with animal caricatures painted in red, black, and white. The other poles, also carved with stylized animals and human figures stood unattached in front of the entrance pole.

I looked back at the trail. Fog still hung on the trees and seemed to separate the world Born of Songs had built in the clearing from everything below, a world I was now in, but not of, that the Haida believe is inhabited by beings like those carved on the poles. The figures seemed alive, watching, and waiting, as if trying to decide what to do with an intruder.

"Grandfather carved them," Jamie said proudly. "Each tells a story of my people's past—and future."

"Past and future?" I asked. "The future hasn't happened. How can it be a story?" I took in each pole and examined their large faces, each of which stared blankly into the distance, seemingly focused on nothing.

Jamie laughed and replied, "My people think time is a circle. Circles don't begin or end. The past bleeds into the future and the future backflows into the past. The present here and now is where they meet. That's what these poles say."

I shook my head. "They don't say anything to me."

"Look closely," she instructed. "Start with the lowest carving on the pole in front of the house. It's a sow grizzly with its belly split open for a door. Bear Mother is my clan's ancestor. Anyone who enters this house returns to her. When they leave, they are reborn."

"Reborn? I still don't follow."

"Be patient and listen. Whatever meaning you find is inside you. Now look at the second carving."

"The one above the sow grizz? Looks like a squatting woman with a small animal sitting on her head. A bear cub?"

Jamie clasped her hands in front of her chin and smiled approvingly. "That's right. Now, do you see the bird with a large beak holding the top of the woman's head in its claws? That's Raven."

"But he has human arms instead of wings folded over what looks like a child holding some sort of disk."

"Yes," she exclaimed approvingly. "Very good! In the Haida story of how the world was created, Raven kidnapped a child from Sky Father's house along with the sun. Do you see the small disk under the other wing? When Sky Father's people came after Raven, he dropped the child into the ocean and kept the sun so the earth could have heat and light."

"What's the child holding?" I asked.

"Again, very good. Your eyes miss little. The child is holding a salmon's dorsal fin. According to the story, after the child was dropped into the ocean, a salmon swam by and he grabbed its dorsal fin. The salmon took the child back to Sky Father's house."

"What about the three men standing on Raven's head? They look like they're wearing stove pipe hats."

"They're the Three Watchmen. They warn when danger comes, just like they warned Sky Father when Raven kidnapped his child and the sun."

"A real thief," I laughed as I pointed my right thumb over my shoulder toward the trail. "We sure could have used a warning back there."

"I knew Bear Mother was watching," she replied coyly. "There was enough warning."

"Guess it doesn't matter now," I replied as I surveyed the remaining poles. "I think I'm beginning to see a pattern."

She snuggled close again. "Take your time. You're just starting."

My curiosity was now overwhelming, like a man born blind who suddenly sees for the first time but isn't sure of what he sees. "That pole on the left—why does it have only one figure carved on the top?"

"It's special," she answered. "Your people might call it a memorial. It's for my clan."

"Your clan is the Bear, so the figure must be a grizzly bear. But why does it have human legs? Is this a human being wearing a bear's skin?"

"Something like that," she said slowly. "We call him Bear Chief."

I glanced back at the entry pole, then refocused on the bear with human legs. "The child Raven kidnapped was his child?"

"No, but his son in human form married Bear Mother. When she took him to her house to meet the Bear People, they were human beings. But they put on their bear coats and became grizzly bears. Except for Bear Mother. She always stayed human."

I shook my head. "Sounds like the fairy tales my mother used to tell me."

Jamie suddenly pulled away. "My people believe animals can be human beings and human beings animals," with a sternness in her voice I had not heard before. "It's all a matter of power and knowing how to use it."

"Whatever the hell that means," I muttered under my breath. "That pole is sure tall. It must be over thirty feet."

She pointed to the pole on the right. "That one's as tall. It's a burial pole. Only dead chiefs—and sometimes shamans—are put in them."

"There's nothing carved on this pole's shaft," I observed. I focused on the five horizontal planks running perpendicular to the burial pole's shaft at the top. A face was carved at the center of the plank. "Another grizzly?" I asked.

"Bear Mother," she answered.

"Look at that snarl. Her teeth look like rip saws."

"She scares away evil from the bodies placed behind the planks."

I breathed out a soft laugh. "Seems a bit late for that, at least for the dead people."

"So much for you to learn and so little time," she retorted. "There are worse things than being dead."

"So I heard." I continued looking at the planks. "Anybody there now?"

"Not yet," she replied in a voice I could barely hear. I looked away from the burial pole at her. She stared at the center totem pole, the largest of the four. I followed her gaze but didn't say anything.

"Tell me what you see," she asked.

"Another grizzly bear on top. He or she is holding something . . . or crushing something . . .between its front paws. Are they human beings?"

"Close," she answered. "They're two bear cubs carved as human beings. According to the story, Bear Mother got pregnant and gave birth to twin cubs. A male and a female. After her relatives found her living with her bear husband in a cave, they killed him and took Bear Mother back to her village. Her cubs took off their bear coats and became human beings. After Bear Mother died, her cubs put their bear coats on again and returned to live with the Bear People."

"Is the next figure a man squatting on the head of a bird?"

"Yes."

"So, what's the story?"

Jamie pointed toward the house. "Come. Grandfather is waiting. He'll answer your question there."

We began walking towards Raven's House, a rectangular structure built of red cedar logs and planks. Four corner posts, each about eight feet high, supported four massive beams angling up to a peak beam twelve feet high. Cedar shakes ran from the center support beam three feet past the lower beams to create eaves running along the northern and southern outer walls. More perpendicular side planks hung from the lower horizontal beams to the ground.

"Good God, a house like this in the middle of nowhere," I exclaimed. "I'd guess about thirty feet wide and fifty feet long." I motioned toward the black faces painted on the outer walls. "Grizz and ravens?" I asked.

"Yes," Jamie replied. "And they're more inside."

We paused at the entry pole. "Your people are sure into bears and birds." I studied the sow grizzly's open belly. There was no door and I saw Born of Songs sitting in front of a small fire at the center of a large single room. Gray puffs of smoke rose lazily through a hole cut directly over the fire pit.

"You say Born of Songs built all this?"

"It took him thirty years, but Raven helped," she whispered. "It's still not finished, but soon. Let's go in." She bent low and passed through the opening.

"This is one strong, unpredictable woman," I thought. Anyone who faces down a sow grizz with cubs she calls "Mother" has got to be taken seriously. I took a deep breath and followed her inside.

A red blanket was draped over Born of Song's shoulders. He wore a coned shaped hat with a wide brim that circled his head above his eyebrows. He reminded me of the watchmen sitting on top of the entry pole.

"Look closely," Jamie whispered. "See where you are and remember."

"Not likely I'll forget," I said.

"Don't be too sure," she said firmly.

It sounded like a warning, but I was too taken up with the house's dimly lit interior to pay much attention. Its empty simplicity was jolting. I expected more carvings and paintings. There were none, except for more ravens and bears carved into the four corner poles. No two were alike, and each stood or sat in different poses, mouths wide open in snarls, as if ready to attack. Shadows cast by the fire danced on the unpainted walls and the corner post figures. A large tin pot rested on a flat rock beside the fire.

Born of Songs sat to the right of an enormous grizzly bear robe with head and claws still attached that hung over an alder stand with a horizontal cross beam lashed near the top. The bear's open mouth clinched a large bone stuck behind four-inch canine teeth. Its front legs, spread wide by the cross beams, seemed to crush an invisible victim.

"Come, sit by the fire," Born of Song said cheerfully, "here where its warm."

I sat and crossed my legs. "Jamie tells me you built all this and carved the totem poles too. I've never seen anything like it."

Born of Songs grinned. "Not even in a book?"

"Sure, in books about Indian culture, and magazines like *National Geographic*. That's nothing like this."

"He's seen a lot, Grandfather," Jamie added. She folded her legs under her hips as she sat beneath the bear hide hanging on the stand.

"Jamie's right about that," I said. "The problem is I don't understand what I've seen. On the way up here, a sow grizz with cubs charged us. It happened fast, and both us should be dead if what I've heard about grizz with cubs is true."

Born of Songs winked at Jamie and grinned. "What you've heard is true, but it's also true that you're both alive. What is there to understand?"

"How Jamie could walk up the sow grizz free as you please and talk to it. She called the grizz 'Bear Mother' and played with the cubs and called them family and got the damned bear's permission for me to be here. You've got to admit, that's unusual."

Born of Songs leaned back, grinned, then replied, "Lucky she was with you."

"No shit," I said angrily. "Then she brings me to your house and these totem poles because she wants me to help Jonathan. Hell, you could have just asked, and by the way, help Jonathan with what?"

"You'll find out soon enough," Born of Songs answered with sudden seriousness. 'If you can help, your reward will be great."

Born of Song's voice was now mellow and friendly, like a salesman making his pitch. He drew a tin box and a long-stemmed pipe from his blanket, opened the box and stuffed a pinch of moist brown tobacco into the pipe's bowl. "Let's smoke first," he said. Then he lit up with a burning stick he drew from the fire, took three quick puffs, and handed the pipe to me.

"Is this my reward?" I asked as I took the pipe.

"It depends. A man deserves what he gets by what he attains," he said slyly. "Take a long drag. It'll relax you."

His eyes seemed covered by a soft glaze. "What the hell is this?" I gagged. I coughed hard and shoved the pipe away. "Burnt rope?"

Born of Songs's laughter broke in waves over the fire circle while Jamie grinned as she lowered her head. "We call it 'tobacco,' at least around strangers." He reached for the pipe and handed it to Jamie. "It's really marijuana. My people have used it for hundreds of years."

"We're smoking pot? That's it," I shouted. "No more games." I jumped to my feet and stumbled toward the door.

"Please, David," Jamie pleaded. "It's not easy for us either."

I stopped and turned around. Her sad dark eyes fixed on me for an instant, then focused on the fire, her hands folded across her lap. Born of Song's laughter disappeared, as if carried by the fire's heat through the smoke hole. "Be warned," he said sternly. "Stay or leave, but either way, you will become a new man or die."

It was like being suspended mid-stride between running and standing in midair, like a cartoon mouse chased by a cat. A force seemed to flow from Born of Songs and connect to something within me, something more than curiosity aroused by a strange old man with a granddaughter who energized my hormones, even as it was like what I experienced with Jamie during the night, and just as powerful, except with her its form was sexual. It had astonished me because through her I seemed to have sensed something like an opening to unnamed realities hidden deep within me that I needed to know. I even thought I might have a similar opening for her. But what I felt flowing from Born of Songs was without form and very scary.

My attention wandered from Born of Songs and Jamie to the carved figures on the corner poles. I was afraid and knew I should be. But I didn't know what I was afraid of, only that I should run like hell. But when I focused on Jamie, my mind found a circle of tranquility like that in the eye of a hurricane. It's always safe in the eye of a hurricane. It's running from the eye that kills. So, I stayed.

Born of Songs shoved more wood on the fire. Cracking sounds echoed through the room as the fire built higher. He offered me the pipe and without protest I took another drag as heat began to ooze throughout my body like melting butter. I inhaled then watched the exhaled smoke merge with the fire smoke as it wrapped the room in silent amber haze.

I returned the pipe to Born of Songs. The burning cedar cracked louder as the room became increasingly warmer, and I took off my coat. My eyes passively followed the grayish smoke, heavy with orange spars and white ash gusting up in a miniature fire storm through the smoke hole. Shadow figures cast around the room by fire light danced like spirits over the walls. Things got blurry fast. I shook my head as I closed my eyes. When that didn't help, I glued my eyes on Jamie. She sat impassively beneath the bear hide, and I noticed a claw was missing from its left front paw. It struck me as strange, and when I tried to ask about it, the words jammed in the back of my throat.

Jamie looked at me, nodded, then closed her eyes and clocked herself in whatever interior vision she was having. Then I picked up the pipe and inhaled another drag. That's when I noticed a single bear claw hanging from a chain between Jamie's breasts. By then, I was sweating hard as the room began a slow spin. Jamie's body and the bear hide seemed to expand and contract in yellow bursts of energy, like lights raised and dimmed by someone working a rheostat. I looked away at the raven and bear figures carved on the corner posts. They seemed to breathe in concert with Jamie, like interchangeable life forms—dead wood carvings shifting to living beings, while human beings transmuted to animals. "See, how easy and natural," the carvings seemed to whisper. "Your mind can shape the world as a river shapes its own banks."

I shut my eyes. Sensations and images still washed in my mind like waves at high tide—Jonathan not wanting to be Haida, lying drunk in the next room while I wrapped myself in Jamie; a sow grizzly bear she called "Mother" that would have killed me if Jamie hadn't asked for my life; totem poles and painted animals on walls; and Born of Songs beginning to tell the story of his people. When I finally opened my eyes, all these memories transfigured into a vision that coalesced time and space and past and future, into a story I watched unfold in my mind as if I were watching a play in the round.

"I will tell you the story of the Haida people and my clan," Born of Songs began. "How the daughter of Bear Mother married a great hunter and bore many sons and one daughter. How my people prospered because they honored Raven and the Bear People. And the games Raven plays that give us life—until now."

7

My first reaction to Born of Song's story was that it had nothing to do with me. But as soon as he finished, weird things began to happen. Smoke and ash boiled over Born of Songs and Jamie, but I wasn't sure if the haze covered them or was only in my head. The surface of their bodies seemed blurred, and I felt sluggish, drained of energy and mad as hell. I closed my eyes and rotated my head from side to side to try and clear my mind.

"You brought me to this place to hear a goddamn fairy tale," I said angrily to Jamie. I opened my eyes and tried to stand. "This is crap!"

Born of Songs doubled over in laughter. "Too late," he giggled. "You can't go anywhere."

He was right. Something knocked me on my back, and I was paralyzed by some sort of force. Through the corner of my right eye, I barely made out Jamie standing up under the bear robe. It seemed to wrap around her body as she stood, as if someone standing behind her was helping her put on a fur coat. The next instant Born of Songs stood directly over my head. His mouth was stretched into a tight humorless grin. He was wrapped in a red blanket with black feathers sown into the edges, and he wore a black bird mask with an enormously straight beak protruding from the top of his forehead. His black eyes glared red beneath the beak and seemed to melt into the painted eyes of the mask.

"What do you see?" Born of Songs demanded. His eyes and the mask's eyes bore into my eyes. "Only a crazy old Indian wearing a mask? Something else, maybe?" he jeered. "Answer," he shouted. "You can speak."

I remembered the totem poles. "You," I shouted, "wearing a raven mask."

Born of Songs reached inside his blanket and pulled out a small drum. "Close enough," he said as he started to beat a slow, even cadence as he danced in small circles above my head, imitating the way a raven prances, his head bobbing up and down and from side to side. As I struggled to move, I saw the boundaries between the old man's head the raven mask dissolve.

Born of Songs stopped chanting when Jamie took it up, slowly at first, in rhythm with the drum. It was the song she sang when she cooked our breakfast, this time in her language, and I understood the words as if I had spoken Haida all my life.

> I have taken a man of beauty
> > for my husband.
> I have taken him from his friends.

By then my body felt stiff as a wooden plank and the only thing I could see was the old man's slow bird movements above my head.

> I hope his kinsmen will not come
> > and take him away from me.
> I will be kind to him.

Heavy steps shuffled from Jamie's direction.

> Berries, berries will I give him from the hill.
> And roots from the ground.

The footsteps stopped and a huge shape loomed over me and blocked Born of Songs from my sight. It was a grizzly bear standing on hind legs. Its claws sliced through the air, five on the left claw and four on the right. The black lips of its snarling mouth curled over five-inch canine teeth. Jamie's song came deep from its throat, soft and as beautiful as the first time she sang it to me.

> I will do everything to please him.
> For him I make this song,
> And for him I will sing it.

I tried to scream, but the sound stayed in my head and rang like an echo through a box canyon. As the echo died, I heard Born of Songs speak. It was his voice, but not his normal voice, more like the squawk of a parrot someone taught to speak. "Too late. You chose. Now I choose you."

I rolled my eyes and looked up. A jet-black bird strutted back and forth near the top of my head, wings spread and glaring through yellow eyes. "You chose. Now I choose you," it repeated over and over again.

"Do not be afraid," Jamie's voice gently whispered through the grizzly's mouth. I heard the bear drop on all fours and felt its wet mouth and black tongue nuzzle my face. "Today, you are reborn," her voice said.

"Today, you are reborn. Today you are reborn," Born of Songs repeated in a parrotlike voice. The raven jumped on my forehead as the grizzly bear tugged at my shirt. "Naked as a new baby," the Raven teased. "This game will be fun."

Whatever held me suddenly released my head as the Raven jumped off. It began strutting in small circles, then picked up a stone and took off lazy in a flight over my body. Then the grizzly bear rose on its hind legs as a savage roar thundered through the cabin. I watched the bear snap at the air before it plunged straight down to my chest. Its four-clawed paw slashed a midline incision in one vertical swipe from my neck to my navel. There was no pain, but I could feel blood seeping warm and sticky over my skin as it pooled on the dirt floor. The surprise of it must have pushed my mind to the top of the room, where I seemed to float like a detached ghost over my bleeding body. I watched the bear spread my chest open, watched the bear devour my internal organs one by one, the way grizzly bears eat favorite parts of a kill. First the stomach, then liver, spleen, lungs, kidneys. As she ate each organ, Raven dropped a rock into its cavity. It wasn't until the grizzly bear flung itself on my heart and ripped it, beating, from my chest that pain seared white hot through my half-devoured body. I howled and screamed, and when the Raven dropped the last stone in my chest, my screams faded into oblivion.

8

"Will he have power, Grandfather?" I heard a woman's voice ask. I blinked and slowly opened my eyes. Jamie and Born of Songs were kneeling over me.

"Who knows?" the old man answered. "It depends on if he had a vision. If he did, he'll dream it again many times. Trouble is, David doesn't believe in visions, only dreams. He'll need convincing." He sounded like a doctor discussing a patient's condition after surgery.

"You will help him," Jamie asserted.

"As my father helped me the first time Raven called my name. David is becoming another man now. He will need our help. But time is short. He must leave with Jonathan to fight in another white man's war."

I tried to sit up. "See, he's coming out of it," Jamie said.

Born of Songs gave me the once-over. "He Whose Voice Is Obeyed must decide. If Raven wants David, his path will be hard."

"Bear Mother will protect him," Jamie muttered.

"Hope is a daylight thing, Granddaughter. Right now, that's all we've got."

Born of Songs and Jamie steadied me as I tried to stand up. "What the hell happened? I'm dizzy and sore as hell."

Jamie massaged the back of my neck. "It'll pass," she said. "Think hard. Do you remember anything?"

"Remember what?" I demanded. My knees buckled as Born of Song held my left arm and steadied me.

"Your people call it a dream," Jamie said. "Did you dream anything?"

"Patience, Granddaughter," Born of Songs instructed. "What we seek can't be hurried."

"There's no time for patience," Jamie shot back. "David, you must remember! Did you have a vision?"

Equilibrium gradually returned. "I don't know. Only vague impressions." I shook free from Born of Songs and stumbled around the fire circle, then stopped and stared at the bear hide. "You and Born of Songs . . . a grizz and a raven . . .there was a song." I turned toward Jamie in sudden recognition. "The one you sang this morning . . . and terrible pain."

"What else?" Jamie asked.

My body twisted tight with remembering. "Something . . . hell, I don't know."

"Enough for now," born of Songs said. "It will come to you in its own time."

"Some dream!" I sputtered.

"Better get back to the cabin," Jamie said. "Grandfather will explain more on the way down."

The thought of leaving Born of Song's place suddenly made me feel better. Things had been too weird, and some were downright too dangerous to be around. Compared to the scary stuff I sensed in these mountains, the war I was about to ship out to suddenly looked good. I was wrong on both accounts. I didn't exactly run out of Raven's House, but I didn't waste any time getting away either. As I stepped into the day, morning sunlight flared painfully in my eyes, and I had to squeeze them shut against the glare. As I began adjusting to the sunlight, I shaded my forehead with both hands and squinted down the trail. Cool westerly wind moaned softly through the forest encircling the clearing. My senses sharpened as I watched a line of cumulus clouds filled with rain roll in from the Gulf of Alaska. The wind picked up and carried the familiar call of a bird circling overhead. I looked up in time to see a large raven land on the head of the grizzly carved on the memorial pole.

"You'll see more of Raven," Born of Songs said as he stood next to me. "It's a good sign."

"Of what?" Raven cries pierced the wind as the bird spread its wings and up drafted high over the clearing. It hung stationary for a moment, then shot over the forest towards Nathan's cabin.

"Of power," Born of Songs answered. "We call Raven 'He Whose Voice is Obeyed.' Keep thinking about your vision," he instructed. "What did Raven do in your dream?"

"Everything's blank," I answered. Jamie moved to my side, and I tried to read her expression for clues. "Just garbled images with lots of blanks," I said. "Nothing makes sense."

"It's all right, David," Jamie said. "Grandfather is right. Understanding can't be forced. It must come in its own time."

"If it comes at all," Born of Songs sighed. There was desperation in Born of Song's voice. I followed his eyes, waiting and not knowing what to do. But I had the feeling nothing was finished and wouldn't be for a long time.

The approaching storm pushed the rain harder through the clearing. "You can smell the rain," Jamie observed.

Born of Songs started hiking, and I followed with Jamie trailing behind. When we reached the tree line he abruptly stopped and spun around. I ran into him and almost knocked him over. But he ignored it and started to talk.

"Many years ago, I had a half-remembered vision I thought was nothing but a dream." His body seemed to take on the suppleness of an excited child. "Just pictures of bears and ravens. My father was a famous shaman and Raven was his spirit guide. He found a way to help me remember my vision, and when I did, I became a shaman for my people. I will help you the same way."

Flapping wings cut through the sky, and I looked up. "Raven has returned," Jamie whispered. The bird began looping figure eights over the center totem pole.

"You mean I'm becoming a Haida shaman? That's bullshit."

"Maybe . . . maybe not," Born of Songs replied. "Could be your vision is a power vision. You and Jonathan can sure use power where you're going. It could also be just a dream, as white people say. You won't know for sure until you remember it. If you don't, your vision is worthless."

"Jamie, what the hell is he talking about? Let's get back to the cabin before we get soaked. At least that makes sense."

"Listen to Grandfather," she said angrily. "Don't be so damned afraid of what you don't understand."

"The trouble is," Born of Songs grumbled, "David wants an easy way that he can control. He wants things as he wants them, not as they are. So, he misses a lot of truth."

The raven played on the updrafts. I glanced back at the eyes of the carved ravens and grizz on the totem pole. The first time I saw them they seemed like threatening guardians protecting the clearing from intruders. But as I glanced back and forth between the circling raven and the totem poles, I felt something different. The carvings I first saw now seemed benign and downright friendly.

"I don't belong here," I said in a loud voice.

A chorus of disembodied male and female voices rose and fell with the gusting wind. "You are here! You belong!"

"Don't belong where?" Jamie asked. "Who are you talking to?"

"Didn't you hear it?"

"Hear what?" She scanned the clearing. "Did you hear anything, Grandfather?"

"Just wind. It sometimes makes strange sounds through the poles."

I wasn't convinced, but I didn't want to argue. "That must be it. Just wind."

"Let's get going," Jamie said impatiently. "The storm's almost on us."

Born of Songs started down the trail. "It might not be the wind," he said. "Everything—birds, animals, trees, wind—speaks its own voice. The trick is learning how to listen." He chuckled like a man getting to the punch line of a joke only he understood. "Hell, maybe the poles were talking to you."

"It was just the wind," I said sharply.

"You sure about that?" Jamie asked.

"Yeah, I'm sure. How come you or your grandfather didn't hear it?"

Born of Songs picked up the pace. "Maybe we weren't supposed to hear it," he said with a sly voice. "Maybe their words were only for you. You must listen to everything: human beings, animals, trees, birds, insects, stones, stars. Everything speaks in its own voice." He stumbled, then caught his balance. "Most of all," he continued, "listen to your heart. You know, what white people call 'feelings.'"

"Do you understand what Grandfather is telling you?" Jamie asked.

"I hear his words, but not his meaning," I answered. More raven squawks drew my attention to the graying sky. "I supposed that damned bird is talking too."

Suddenly Born of Songs stepped off the trail and stopped, and my momentum pushed me past. "What the hell now," I grumbled. "More voices?" I turned around and faced uphill.

"It'll be hard teaching him," Born of Songs said to Jamie. "Harder than we thought. He doesn't want see the world like we do."

Jamie shook her head. "Yes, Grandfather," she replied. "Maybe it was wrong to try."

"Maybe so," I said angrily. "All I know is I'm hungry, tired, cold, and Jonathan and I will leave for a war early tomorrow. Bur right now, all I want to do is haul ass back to the cabin before the damned storm hits."

"You're also confused," Born of Songs added. "Boundaries between the things you thought you knew got suddenly blurred. What you think is real may not be. What you think isn't real may be." He glanced up at the circling raven and smiled. "That happened to me too. Many years ago when Raven and Bear Mother made me into a shaman."

That's when my dream flashed back into my mind, and I remembered. "You had the same dream . . . the same nightmare?"

Born of Songs eyes flashed the color spectrum as he replied, "We call it a vision, but your vision and mine are not the same. No two visions are alike. But Raven and Bear Mother called me in a vision. They are my spirit helpers. Maybe they called you too."

"It's true," Jamie quickly added. "It's rare, even for a Haida. But if it was really a vision, you must not run from it."

"This is unbelievable," I snapped. "Called? To be a shaman? Hell, I don't even know what that means."

Disappointment washed over Jamie's eyes, and she turned away, trying to hide the sadness that edged her face. "You said you wanted to learn about my people. Did you mean it? Were your words empty?"

Born of Songs spoke before I could answer. "If you let it, maybe your vision will instruct you. But be careful. A vision can kill if you don't let it teach."

Before I could reply, pictures began flashing on and off in my mind, like a flashlight flickering on and off on a dark night to get someone's attention.

"I remember being torn apart by a grizzly bear," I said. "And the damned thing was singing as it ripped open my chest. And I recognized the song. Jamie sang it this morning."

"Hurry before you lose it," Born of Songs of Songs ordered. "What else?"

"No chance of losing it now. You were in it too," I said to Born of Songs. "You were playing a drum and dancing. You wore a raven mask and spoke in raven noises."

"Anything else?" Jamie asked.

"Pain, as a raven dropped hot stones on my open chest. That's all, except coming to with both of you kneeling over me, flat on my back and used up like a roller towel in a Mexican men's room."

I looked up at the raven circling lazily overhead in the cold thermals as more images flashed in and out of my mind. The raven began to call again in long, loud shrills. The sounds echoed in my head like the sound of my own voice. I felt my body becoming weightless and the wind began to pick me up. I felt myself slip away from solid ground into the updrafts and I began soaring with the raven, like a passenger in a glider. Then the raven stopped its cries. Except for the wind rushing past, there was no sound as we glided up and down in the raven's flight path. Then the raven seemed to laugh like a clown playing tricks on a friend as it called out, "Look what we can do, look what we can do," like a child playing a new game.

I laugh hysterically with the raven as we flew over Jamie and Born of Songs. I was in Raven's game, seeing what it saw, feeling what it felt, bound by nothing except empty sky. Then suddenly, the raven straightened its flight path and dove down the trail towards Born of Songs cabin. Jonathan stood on the porch looking up as we flew past.

"It's Jonathan, it's Jonathan!" I shouted. "My God, it's Jonathan!" The surprise of it must have broken my concentration, because at that instant my body's weight pressing my feet into the wet earth replaced the sensation of flight. I opened my eyes. "I flew with the raven," I whispered. "I really flew with the raven." Jamie walked slowly toward me. Her warmth spread over me as I pulled her close. "Will I fly again?" I asked.

"That and more," she beamed.

"I still don't get it," I said to Born of Songs.

Born of Songs shook his head as he smiled in relief. "Understanding comes with time," he replied quietly. "A whole lot of time. Raven and Bear Mother will clear up everything when the time is right. What you saw is only the beginning. What you need now is patience."

Jamie pressed closer. "Patience isn't one of my long suits," I said.

"Let's get going," Born of Songs demanded.

And about an hour later, as we approached the cabin, we saw Jonathan standing on the porch listening to the thunderclaps rumbling through the flint gray afternoon sky as he watched us run out of the forest into the clearing through sheets of rain. Halfway across the clearing, Jamie stumbled. I reached back and caught her, and we continued running hand in hand, laughing like children.

Born of Songs was close behind. Just before we reached the porch, Jonathan staggered into the cabin and plopped onto the couch.

"You run fast for an old man," I puffed at Born of Songs. "You're not even breathing hard."

Born of Songs chuckled. "Old shamans know how to conserve energy."

"Are you OK?" I said to Jamie.

"Turned my ankle a little," she replied. "I just need to walk it off."

"I need a drink. Where's the booze?" Jonathan complained.

"Better get out of these clothes," Jamie said. She walked toward the bedroom. "Then I'll fix some supper."

"For Christ's sake, why are you wearing that?" Jonathan called out to Jamie. Jamie ignored him and entered the bedroom.

"Can I help?" I called out.

Jamie chuckled and said, "I can change my own clothes, thank you."

"I meant with supper."

"Help Grandfather build up the fire in the stove. There's dry wood on the porch."

"I don't want to eat," Jonathan sputtered. "I want a drink," he said as he jumped to his feet, lost his balance, and fell back on the couch.

"You need food, not booze," Born of Songs said. "There'll be no more booze tonight. Booze steals your soul." Then he slapped my back. "This time, the Haida are taking a white man's soul."

"Is that what's happening?" I asked. I rummaged through my duffel pulled out a change of clothes.

Born of Songs started to undress. "Something like that," he said. "Now you have two souls—white and Haida. You'll have to figure out for yourself how to put them together."

"Tell me how," I said as I draped my wet shirt across the back of a chair near the fireplace.

"I can't," he replied. "Your vision must teach you."

Jonathan tried to stand again by tightening his legs and stiff-arming the back of the couch. "What the hell are you two talking about?" he fumed.

Born of Songs tossed his wet pants in a heap near the fireplace. "David is your brother now." He opened an old cedar plank chest and pulled out a pair of faded Levies and a brown wool shirt. "Raven and Bear Mother gave him a vision."

Jonathan squinted at me. "What the hell's this old coot talking about, man?"

"Like he said, I had a vision."

"What kind of vision?" Jonathan steadied himself on the back of the couch. "The only visions I have come from booze."

"I'll tell you later if I can. When you sober up." I started walking barefoot toward the porch.

"Jesus H. Christ," I heard Jonathan hiss. "What did you do, old man? Adopt him?"

"Not me, Raven and Bear Mother."

"Are you saying he's a shaman? For Christ's sake, he's a white man. Does David believe this crap?"

"Things aren't always what they seem," I said. I carried a load of alder from the front door to the wood box by the fireplace. I gazed into the fire, focused on nothing.

"Did you have another vision?" Born of Songs asked.

"Maybe," I said as I knelt and shoved wood into the low burning fire. "I'm not sure."

Jonathan kicked the back of the couch and punched a table. "Bullshit!" he cursed.

"It doesn't matter," I said. "Whatever's coming will be hard on both of us."

"David is your friend, Jonathan Blue Heron," Born of Songs murmured. "Now he's your brother."

"Then maybe he'll find me some booze."

That night Jamie sat on the floor in front of the fireplace, wrapped in a blanket, listening to droplets of rain running down the chimney and hissing on the amber coals, to Jonathan's snoring filtered through the heavy rain peppering the cabin's shake roof, and to her own thoughts and emotions competing for attention with the external sounds of the world. She looked down at David, stretched out beside her in sleep, then silently rose and glided toward the bedroom. She carefully parted the curtain and peered inside. Born of Songs was sleeping on his back next to Jonathan, wrapped in an old brown quilt on its last legs.

"Grandfather's time is running out," she softly whispered to herself. "So is Jonathan's. I hope Grandfather's right about David."

She studied Jonathan. He was asleep on his stomach, face down on a pillow. "Why can't you be what you are, Brother?"

She heard movement behind her, then a whisper. "Jamie?"

"Here," she answered. She quickly wiped her eyes with the edge of her blanket and slipped beside David. "Just checking on Grandfather and Jonathan."

David stretched and yawned. "Are they OK?"

"I worry about Grandfather. He's getting old, and as for my brother . . ."

He drew her deep into the blankets. "His time isn't finished," he assured her. "I don't know how I know, but I do."

"Grandfather tried to help our people." Then she corrected herself. "Your people, now. He tries to hold us together, but it's slowly killing him."

"And Jonathan?"

"He's the problem," she said bitterly. "He cuts himself off from this land and his people. He's lost his spirit. That's why he drinks."

"I understand," David replied.

"I think you do."

David turned on his back. In the dim light, he could make out four parallel lines running from his sternum to the middle of his belly. "I wish to hell I could understand all this."

She caressed his chest and tried to reassure him. "You don't have to understand now. Just remember this day. You'll recognize it later."

He put his hands on her hips and rolled her towards him. She rolled willingly, and David wondered what else she thought about.

9

The fog was so thick when I pulled off the road that I had to wait it out until early the next morning. By that time, I could see that I had parked on an elbow of land overlooking Cache Creek. Somewhere deep in the valley a raven called. I sat up and listened, then slowly crawled from my sleeping bag and out my pickup's tailgate into a sunrise that laced over the Western coast range and burnet pale fingers of light into the wispy ground fog.

There were chores, and I hurried through them: reheating last night's leftover coffee, rolling up my sleeping bag and stowing it away, rummaging through the food box for a bag of freeze-dried apples and pears. The raven called again, louder and closer, as I poured cold water over my head from a plastic jug. I wiped my face and listened to the raven's cry echoing south to north. It sounded like a hurry-up call to get back on the road.

I didn't need coaxing. I tightened the cap on the water jug, poured some barely warm coffee into a tin cup, and ate fast. Ten minutes later, I took one last look around, slammed the tailgate shut, and climbed into the cab and started the engine. My tires squealed as I pulled onto the highway towards Prince Rupert, thinking about ravens and grizzly bears, and that morning Jonathan and I left for Vietnam.

Jamie and I woke between storm fronts and the night's last moonlight streaming through the cabin's front window, bundled up in silence against the damp cold, trying not to think of anything. When thinking could no longer be avoided, Jamie brushed her lips across mine and whispered, "It's almost daybreak."

I stretched and pulled her close. "Just say the word, and I'll desert. The Army will never find me in these mountains."

"You can't, you won't, and you know it." Her voice was plaintive as she pulled away and gazed into my eyes. "You and my brother are on a journey. There's no going back. Maybe later, when everything's finished, you'll come back."

"Count on it," I promised as I sat up. "I'll bring us both back from this damned war in one piece."

She shook her head. "Vietnam will not be your only war. You are a warrior now for the rest of your life. That means knowing you can die and accepting the fact. Only then can you tell the difference between what's real and what's not when death covers you like your own skin—in Vietnam and in other places—in more ways than you can know."

I only half-heard what she said because I was focused on the morning's light glowing in her dark eyes. Passion overcame good sense and I blurted, "I love you."

It set her back. I didn't expect that. I had never said it to any woman before, and I wanted her to accept it for what I took to be face value. All she did was frown and say, "Now is not the time."

"I don't see why not, especially after what's happened between us."

"Before there's an 'us' much more must happen."

I pouted and stared at the ceiling, a disappointed and inexperienced young man unable to comprehend a woman's gift given without strings. "So, all we've done is screw ourselves silly," I muttered under my breath. I knew it was a mistake the moment I opened my mouth.

"Much more than sex needs to pass between us," she said. Her lips quivered as fury blazed from her eyes. "You cheapen everything," she fumed. "What you call 'love' has little to do with that's happening here."

That infuriated me and I pulled her to me. She stiffened, then relaxed. "It depends on what you mean by the word, doesn't it," I said. "Why are you afraid of the word? You've said everything else: want, need, like, and assorted drivel. It's all the same. If you don't want to hear the word, I won't use it. Besides, if this white man can have Indian visions, this white man can love an Indian woman who gave then to him."

"Who knows?" she said. "First, we've got to find out how all this will end. This means you must follow your vision's path to the end."

"Guess that'll have to do for now."

"It'll have to," she replied. "Grandfather and Jonathan will be awake soon. You must be hungry, and I know they will be. It's time to start breakfast."

I released her and she started to dress. My belly knotted with disappointment as her nakedness vanished behind a pair of faded Levies and a red and black plaid shirt. I stood and reached for my clothes: a class-A-spit-and-polish-ready-for-inspection-reporting-for-duty-sir! Army uniform.

"How can I follow a path I don't understand," I asked.

Jamie shoved wood into the cook stove and slapped the iron door shut. Its sound cracked through the cabin like a rifle shot. "Sure is cold in here. Why don't you build up the fireplace?"

I pulled four pieces of alder from the fire box and placed then on the coals. "It seems like I've been turning myself on and off in someone else's game since I got here."

Jamie set a large frying pan on the stove and dropped in four slices of ham. "It's not easy knowing that you and Jonathan are going to war today," she said sadly. "That's a game I wish you didn't have to play. Where do you go from here?"

"Back to Ketchikan. Your brother and I have to report to Ft. Lewis in Washington State by tomorrow night. The next day we fly out from McChord Air Force Base with a bunch of replacements. We'll be cutting it close."

"Will you be stationed together?"

"We've been assigned to a firebase near some place called An Loc."

"I've never heard of it."

"Me neither, until we got our orders. Word is, it's a bad place."

Jamie set the coffee pot to brew and started to scramble some eggs. "At least you can watch out for each other."

The ham and eggs sizzled, and the aroma mixed with the coffee's strong hickory smell spreading like vapor through the warming cabin. "Can I do anything to help?" I asked.

She pointed to a stack of dishes on a shelf next to the stove. "You can bring me some plates. Everything's almost done."

I encircled her from the back with my arms and gently kissed the nape of her neck. "God, I'm hungry," I said.

"So am I," Born of Songs said sharply as he pushed through the bedroom curtain.

I let Jamie go and grabbed four plates and set them near the stove. "Good morning," I said sheepishly. "Is Jonathan still unconscious?"

Born of Songs's face was split open at the jaw by a large grin. "He sure as hell wishes he was." He poured a cup of coffee, carried it to the table and sat. "My grandson tied one on too hard last night. Now he staggers around like a man looking into his own grave."

"Maybe he is," Jamie said with a deep sadness.

"Maybe breakfast will help," I suggested. "He hasn't eaten much since we got here. From what you said, he's in for a long trip to Ft. Lewis."

"In more ways than he knows," Born of Songs said. He got suddenly serious and focused on me. "And what about you, friend of my grandson?" He nodded at Jamie and winked. "And my granddaughter?"

"Good as can be expected. At least for someone who's about to go to war after the weirdest furlough anyone's ever had."

"You have power, now," Born of Songs said in a voice barely loud enough to hear. "Don't fight what Raven and Bear Mother have given you. Relax and let your vision work things out."

"That's what Jamie said. It'd sure as hell be easier if I had some idea about how things are supposed to work out."

"If you knew that, you wouldn't need power and we wouldn't need you." Something heavy fell to the bedroom floor. Nathan cocked his head, listened, and then whispered, "Trust your power. It will grow. And when you get to the white man's war, keep your head down. That's all you can do."

Jonathan staggered into the room. "Man, my head feels like a boil and my mouth is drier than an armpit in hell. Just give me some coffee."

Jamie shoved a plate of ham and eggs in front of him as he sat down at the table. "If your skin was any drier, you'd be dead. Eat something. You've got a long trip ahead, and a fast one, according to David."

"All right, Mother," Jonathan whined. "Just lay off, Sis."

"Here's your coffee." She pulled out a chair next to me and began to eat. Jonathan slowly lifted his cup of coffee to his lips with shaking hands and carefully slurped. "This ought to jump start my heart. Thanks, Little Sister."

"Jamie told me your people live in the Queen Charlottes," I said to Born of Songs.

Jonathan suddenly jumped to his feet. "Little Sister's right," he shouted as he walked into the bedroom. "We've got us a long day. Soon as I pack my duffel, we're out of here."

Jamie and Born of Songs didn't want to talk after that. But I still had more questions than I knew how to ask. So, I randomly asked about whatever popped into my head. "Your grandfather lives mostly alone in these mountains to preserve the Haida Way, and Jonathan doesn't like it?" I asked Jamie.

"That's an understatement," she answered.

"How do you preserve the Haida Way?"

"By living in a dumpy apartment near the waterfront in Ketchikan, working in an Indian school. Most of the kids are Haida, and I teach them about their heritage."

"Why was Raven's House built so far from your people's land?" I asked Born of Songs. "Couldn't you do more good living with your people?"

The old man rolled his eyes. "Listen carefully," he said. "I'm Raven's and Bear Mother's shaman. This doesn't fit in living around white people— or other Haida, for that matter. People want us to be saints."

"That's a problem?" I asked.

"Sure is. No shaman can be a saint. There's no choice. We must feel all the ups and downs, happiness and suffering, magic and reality of our people. We must sink as low as a bug and fly as high as an eagle for our people. If we don't do that, we're no damn good to anyone."

"That still doesn't answer my question. How can you do any of that if you don't live with your people?"

Born of Songs frowned. "A shaman's power never lets him fit in. Even among his own people." He rubbed his chin searching for more explanation. "It's like the way your people want preachers to be perfect."

"But what's that got to do with living alone in this place?"

"Everything. What your people call 'sin' makes the world go round. But a shaman must dive like a raven into the middle of life's whirlwind. We must experience all forms of life, and this means not being afraid to cut up and be a fool now and then. That's—what do your people say?—holy too."

"That's a hard way to live," I said. "You must be very lonely."

A faint smile traced across Born of Song's lips. "Lots of quiet, but never alone." He poured another cup of coffee and refilled my cup. "Listen carefully and remember," he instructed. "Nothing's perfect. Not nature, not the Great Spirit, not anything. Even Raven and Bear Mother have good and bad sides. Sometimes, the bad sides give more knowledge than the good sides." He took a breath and sipped his coffee, and then said, "The Forest Service lets me stay here. This is grizz country, and they think the grizz need protecting. I guide them to the best places to study bears and help them track poachers."

"What about Raven's House?" I asked.

"I stay there most of the time. The Feds don't know about it."

"Come on," I grumbled. "They must know. Planes and helicopters fly over these mountains all the time."

Born of Songs winked at Jamie. "That's Raven's problem, not mine."

"Jamie, what the hell does he mean?"

"Grandfather can tell you better than I," she said.

"So, one of you tell me, damn it," I demanded.

"The Feds fly over all the time. I've seen hikers walk around the totem poles and Raven's House and not see anything. Raven makes them blind. Pretty tricky for a bird," Born of Songs chortled.

"The Haida Way lives in there, in that little piece of the world," Jamie added.

My mind was as black as tar as a sense of tragedy filled me like thunderbolts from Kansas. "Come on you two," I said urgently. "Stop jerking me around. Raven's magic or not, someone . . . a Fed, a hiker, a developer from Hell . . . is bound to get wind of it."

"Nothing lasts forever," Jamie replied firmly. "Not the Haida, not your people, nothing."

"Then maybe Jonathan is right," I replied. "Why hang on so hard to a way of life that's dying?"

Born of Songs leaned over the table. "It's one thing when something dies naturally, in its time. It's something else when a thing is murdered."

"This is why we fight," Jamie added. "It's not only the Haida Way, it's the way the world is."

"Hell, death is just the end of life," I retorted. "Nothing else."

Born of Songs slapped the table in disgust and leaned back in his chair. "White people!" he exclaimed in exasperation. "Your people spend all your time running from death and create more death than the world can stand. That's why you and my grandson are leaving for Vietnam. You both think death is just the end of life. Nothing to it. So, it's easy to kill people you don't know or understand. Killing makes white people feel alive."

I pushed back from the table and jumped to my feet. "I didn't choose to go to Vietnam. I've never killed anyone, and I don't want to."

"You've chosen, all right," Born of Songs shot back. "You and Jonathan will kill and be killed."

A chill raced up my spine. "Don't you mean, 'kill or be killed?'" I shot back.

"There are as many ways to live as there are to die." Born of Songs nodded towards the bedroom. "Think of it. In all this beautiful universe, only the earth is a blot. The ocean is a cup of death, and the land is a bloody altar stone. One morning, you will wake up in terror, eat in hunger, and go back to sleep with a mouthful of blood. This happens to all living things. It's the way of all things. But the most terrible form of death is to be alive when your spirit is dead."

Jamie reached for my hand. I looked down and saw sunlight glistening in the slight moister trapped in her eyes. "You and my grandson will come home alive in a year," Born of Songs predicted. "But your spirits will die several times. That's worse than death in battle."

Depression oozed over my mind like a black ink wash. "You two have sure complicated my life. I don't need that. Going to Vietnam is complication enough."

"At least it's not boring," Born of Songs laughed. "If you lead a boring life, chances are you'll face a boring death."

"You talk about Jonathan and me getting killed like it's already happened."

Born of Songs's mouth twisted into a tight frown. "It has, to everything, always, everywhere. Weren't you listening? Remember your vision. Let it teach you how to live and die at the same time."

My depression mutated to rage. "Damn it! Is everything a game with you?" I shouted at Born of Songs. I glared at Jamie. "And with you?"

"Of course," she replied calmly. "The world's a game still being played. When the game stops, the world stops." She rose and started to clear the table. Her face was locked into the detached expression of someone knowing a certain truth. "If you don't know the rules of the game, and where you fit in, you can't play. You just die." She carried a load of dishes to the sink. "Listen to Grandfather's lesson," she instructed, "and let your vision be your teacher."

"I need time I don't have," I replied as Jonathan barged from the bedroom, dressed in his class-A uniform, his duffel bag slung over his right shoulder. "The only time is now," Jonathan barked, "and it's time to go."

"I see you've recovered," Born of Songs said.

"You haven't looked this good since basic," I added.

"Sweet Jesus, you're right," Jonathan said happily. "What do you think, Sis?"

"Not bad for a drunk Indian," Jamie answered sarcastically.

"Well, I'm sober now," Jonathan said as he headed to the front door. "Let's go, man, this Indian wants to kick some yellow commie ass."

Jamie threw her arms around my neck. "Remember your vision," she whispered again. "And keep your head down."

10

I passed the Prince Rupert's city limits sign at noon, impatient as a dog at the sight of a leash. Impatience became irritation as I worked through slow tourist traffic toward the harbor. Near the ferry turnoff I cut a sharp right and stopped beside a phone booth in front of a run-down café. So much more to come. When will it end and who would remember? The only thing pain leaves is a shadow. Not always in the flesh, but always in the mind. I slammed the phone booth door shut as I searched my pockets for change. I found a Canadian quarter and dropped it in the slot and dialed Jamie's number. I impatiently listened to her line ring, and just when I started to hang up, she answered.

"Hello, is that you, David?"

"It's me," I said. "I'm at the ferry terminal on the Rupert side."

"Sorry I took so long to answer," she said breathlessly. "I just got back from work. You made good time."

"I'll be at your place in an hour. I would have made it sooner, but—"

"Don't say anything now," she broke in. "Stay where you are and get us a room. There's a dumpy motel near the terminal called 'The Blue Spruce.'"

"I can see it from here."

"I'll meet you there as soon as I can. Probably in a couple of hours. We need to talk. We can head for Grandfather's place in the morning."

"Good," I replied. "That'll give me some time to clean up. Right now, I feel like I've been rode hard and put away wet."

She laughed, and my God it sounded good. "You still have your sense of humor," she said.

"Seems like I've lost everything else," I replied.

"Soon, David. It will be finished soon."

"That's comforting," I replied. "We've been on this trail too long." Her breath softly whistled through the receiver. "See you when you get here."

I hung up and walked back to my pickup. Images of the past still raced through my head, as if trying to catch up to the present. It was frustrating and fascinating at the same time. My life felt like a hurry-and-catch-up waiting game. College, the Army, Vietnam, Jonathan, Born of Songs, and Jamie. I always seem to be waiting for endings that never come. Yet what was happening was astonishing, and I wasn't ready for it: the amount of unfulfilled time, the long parentheses of nothing between doing one thing and the next. And time white as sound. I climbed into the pickup, drove to The Blue Spruce, and pulled in under a car port next to the manager's office. A blind man wouldn't have missed The Blue Spruce. It was painted tourist green and stuck out like a boil.

A bald, heavy-set man in his midfifties leaning over the registration desk glanced up as I opened the door. He rolled a stubby cigar in his mouth and went back to his conversation with a stocky woman dressed in a red, worn-out housecoat covered with white lilies. Thick, horned-rimmed glasses were pushed to the end of his nose, and he wore a tan shirt unbuttoned halfway down his chest.

"I need a room for the night for two," I said.

The manager turned from the woman and straightened. "Thirty-five a night," he said as he shoved a registration form in front of me. "In advance." He coughed hard as he expelled jets of inhaled smoke over the form. I filled it out and plopped thirty-five US dollars on the desk.

The manager frowned. "You're from the States. You got change coming as soon as I figure the exchange rate."

He reached for his calculator, but I had enough of him. "Forget it," I said. "Just give me the key. We'll be leaving in the morning."

"Suit yourself," the manager mumbled. "Number 12. Just leave the key on the dresser when you leave."

I backed my pickup in front of a first-floor room with the number 12 nailed in black on an oxidized white door, took my .45 from under the seat, climbed down, walked to the rear end, dropped the tail gate, and then hauled out my duffel bag and Winchester. I unlocked the room's door and hesitated out of habit. In Nam you tossed in a grenade before you entered an empty room and scanned right to left before you went in.

I tossed my stuff on a single double bed covered in an off-white spread that smelled of musk.

Red drapes were drawn tight over a single window facing the parking lot, as if to hide the room's secrets from the outside world. Cold air mixed with stale disinfectant and mildew reminded me of a cave. A sudden burst of sunlight brushed butterscotch gold through the open door over a worn-out brown carpet. The room was paneled in dark walnut and furnished with a single oak table, two nightstands, and a suitcase stand in an alcove on the right side of the closet. The bed faced a television set with a sign marked "free cable" in red and blue letters. I switched the wall fan under the window to "high," set the heat to "low, and went out and locked my pickup.

Footsteps clopped unevenly down a breezeway three doors away. A tall, slightly built man with a thick red moustache walked by with an Indian woman wrapped in a long overcoat. She eyed me suspiciously and the man was leery. "Afternoon," he muttered as they passed.

"Afternoon," I replied and watched them disappear into the office. I returned to my room, shut the door, and sat on the bed. "I'm tired of looking for the meaning of things," I once told Jamie one summer in her apartment in Ketchikan. It was after my third year at Stanford and one year after I came home from Vietnam. She always asked lots of questions about Vietnam, and always pressed hard about what happened to me and Jonathan.

"Don't look so hard," she once told me. "Let meaning come."

"I was there," I said, "and I don't understand any of it. I have no idea where meaning comes from."

"From the past," she asserted with innocent certainty.

"The only thing the past is good for is leaving it behind," I said.

"Where did you learn that? At Stanford?"

"In Nam," I said bitterly.

Then she asked a question that stood me up like an uppercut to the chin. "Do you want to leave our past behind?"

Sure as hell, I didn't want that. Anything except that. When I didn't answer, she laughed and said, "Grandfather is right. People secrete meaning the way honeybees secrete wax."

"Even Jonathan?" I blurted.

"Even my brother. Some places and times just exist. That's their meaning."

"You want to know what it was like?" I exclaimed angrily. "OK, damn it! Born of Songs told me a story that made me crazy before the war made me crazier. Now it's your turn. If you can figure it out, let me know."

"We both take a chance," she said softly. "It will change both of us."

Once I decided to tell her about the war, I didn't know how. "Where do I start? Most of the time my mind is still there, even after being home for two years. It's still mostly a blur."

"Start with that and go from there," she said. "Don't force anything."

I settled back, closed my eyes, and started rambling about whatever came to mind. "Mostly, it was like being a spectator at a game. Come to think about it, that's the way it's been since I met you and Born of Songs. Nam was a politician's game. My mistake was trying to play by their rules."

"What do you mean?"

"Before I got there, I thought I knew what the war was about. Stop the Communists. Simple as that, I thought. But after the first day, I found out that no one knew what was going on. Then it was too late. I just had to play along. There wasn't any other choice."

"Did Jonathan feel the same?" she asked.

"He knew it was a phony war before we got there. But he liked it. He really did. He was the only grunt pounding the bush who did. To me, it was like crash landing on a different planet. The feeling got real intense at night."

"How's that?"

"The jungle sounds suddenly stopped. No fading down. Just gone in an instant as if someone gave the signal. Bats, birds, monkeys, snakes, insects picking up a frequency someone born in a jungle might be conditioned to hear but left us wondering about what we weren't hearing."

"What did you do?"

"I tried to turn the outside silence into a mental space to fill with everything I thought was quiet in me. I heard impossible things. Trees breathing, fruit sweating, bugs crawling over rotting vegetation, the heart beats of tiny animals."

I watched Jamie trying to frame my words with mental pictures as she tried hard to take it in. Born of Songs and Jamie had told me stories of Raven, Bear Mother, and the Haida. And I took them in, made them part of me, mostly against my will. As I look back, I figure she thought it was time to reciprocate, imagine what I went through, and make it part of her.

"I learned how to keep it up for a long time, either until the jungle starting shrieking again, or until something familiar brought me out of it, like a helicopter flying overhead, or the ritual your brother followed every morning. He'd wake up, stretch, stagger to the nearest water, wash his face, hack, and spit, tighten his belt, break wind, scratch his legs, finger comb his hair, drink from his canteen, belch, spit again, and sit down. Then he'd always say, 'God, that felt good.' I guess men living uncivilized lives do about the same things when they wake up."

"It didn't keep Jonathan sane," she said.

"We all went crazy in our own way. Although come to think of it, your brother got a head start on the rest of us. Only a certifiably insane man would do more than one tour. I think he was afraid to come home and face what he'd become."

That stiffened her. "I can understand about Jonathan, but what could do that to you?"

"You name it," I answered. "Everyone there got changed from what they were. Everyone I knew, except Jonathan, counted the days of their tour like a gambler counts his cards. They wanted to go home—go anywhere except where they were. What did it for me was Sergeant Lawrence T. Adams. A racist sonofabitch, that one. He ran our platoon and made Jonathan walk point on every operation."

"Why's that?" Jamie whispered.

"Because Jonathan is Haida. Adams told him Indians are natural born scouts. You can guess how that set with Jonathan."

"Yes, I can. What did my brother do?"

"He told Adams to go straight to hell and that he wanted to be treated no differently than a white man. Adams just laughed and said your brother's skin was too dark to be treated like a white man, and that an Indian was nothing but a low-class negro. So, Jonathan jumped Adams and tried to kill him. He almost succeeded, except Adams managed to pull a knife and slash your brother across the face before we could break it up. No charges were filed, but Adams gave Jonathan every dirty job he could think of. On every patrol mission, he ordered Jonathan to walk point so that the VC might kill him. I reported Adams to the platoon commander and wound up walking point with Jonathan on every operation."

"My brother's been on the warpath a long time," Jamie said. "He took you with him."

"Maybe," I said, "except he got off on it."

"I don't understand."

"He learned to like walking point. In fact, he got downright creative about it. I mean, he was always up front with no one giving him orders. And the platoon depended on him to get them through anything bad. They certainly trusted him more than Adams, and with good reason. Jonathan was very good. He knew it and felt important, I think, for the first time in his life. And he actually convinced himself that the war in Vietnam would turn him into a white man."

"That's strange, even for my brother," Jamie said.

"I guess he thought killing Vietnamese Communists would make him white. The black guys in the platoon tried to set him straight. But things really got complicated when he heard Haida voices. Mostly, he heard them at night."

Color drained from Jamie's cheeks. "He dreamed?" she asked.

"From what he told me, they were terrible dreams. Mostly about animals and the ghosts of people he killed. One dream in particular kept cropping up like a piece of shrapnel that takes years to work itself out. He crossed a field covered with Vietnamese dead bodies with a guide who made him get down on all fours and look at them up close. He told me they were powdered with dust and covered in blood. Some of the bodies were blown out of their pants. Some were naked. Then the guide turned into a bear and waved at the bodies with its front paws. When Jonathan looked at the bodies again, he saw the faces of his dead ancestors. There were other dreams, but that one followed him everywhere. It scared him so bad he tried to stay drunk. That was the only time he didn't dream."

Jamie set her jaw tight and asked, "It never dawned on him to listen?"

"He hates being Haida too much to do that. 'Listen to the dream, man,'" I said. "It's a good thing to be a Haida man. Trying not to be will either kill you or people around you or both. Not listening will make you crazier than you already are. Hell, the only thing he did was scream obscenities. The last time I brought it up he tried to crack my skull with a trench shovel."

"See, you have secreted meaning," her voice trembled. "Sometimes what things meaning is painful."

"I sure didn't keep my promise."

"What promise?"

"Don't you remember? It was on the day before we left for Nam. I promised to bring us both back in one piece. You sure as hell called it. It was a promise I couldn't keep."

"Nothing's played out yet," she replied. "What will you do until it is?"

"I want to drop everything and stay with you."

Jamie looked away and said, "The time's not right. You're not ready to live in my world, and I'm not ready to live in yours."

"You keep saying that," I muttered. "It's getting damned old."

She lowered her eyes the way she always did when she shut herself off from things that couldn't be helped. We did it differently in Nam. Whenever things got out of control, we just said, "It don't mean nothin." Trouble was, it never worked when it came to my feelings about Jamie. Instead, I said to myself, "Guess I'll go back to Stanford and finish up. Maybe go to graduate school and focus on animal behavior." Then another idea struck me funny. and I started to laugh.

"What's so funny?" Jamie asked.

"Think I'll study grizzly bears," I said as I giggled.

"She laughed with me and asked, "Why do that? Grandfather and I can teach you everything you need to know about grizzly bears. Besides, the grizz adopted you."

"That's Indian knowledge," I retorted. "I need scientific knowledge."

"See," she teased, "you aren't ready to live in my world."

Jamie spoke the truth and the memory brought me back to the present. "She'll be here soon," I said to the room's emptiness. I pulled my shaving kit from the duffel bag and went into the bathroom. I undressed and tossed my clothes on the floor. "It'll be over soon," I said to my reflection in the mirror. "Then what?" I tried to read an answer from the stubbled reflection looking back at me. Born of Songs was right about one thing. The older we get the more we look like the land. In the end, we become part of the land with a face like a plowed field. I stepped into the shower stall and turned on the water. The shock of the rapidly warming water stung my chest like hot needles. I soaped down, then leaned against the tiled wall and let warm water steam over me. And I thought hard about Jonathan Blue Heron.

Jonathan was shipped back to the States after his third tour. The war's abnormalities freed him from the myths and social restrictions of Haida culture. His enemies became external, tangible, and real, out there beyond the barbed wire of the firebase and his Haida culture. These enemies could be killed, and he focused on them to keep Haida spirits at bay. But after a while, the spirits that warred with him started to ambush him while he as awake, sometimes on point in the bush, sometimes during a firefight, sometimes lying around in our hooch, and once with a Saigon hooker. He never knew when the haunting would come and no one except me knew what was bothering him. And everyone including me thought he was one schizoid nutjob we hoped wouldn't get us killed.

Billy Joe and I told him to go on sick leave. He told us to go to hell. Jonathan never slept unless alcohol induced. When he was awake, he concentrated on whatever enemies the Army supplied him. He happily killed them, for which he was awarded a Silver Star, two Bronze Stars, and at the beginning of his third tour, a promotion to staff sergeant with his own platoon. But the American pullout in 1975 shattered all that. He was unceremoniously plucked out of a firefight and dropped off in San Francisco, discharged him from service as they told him, "You're not needed anymore," and released into a society disillusioned by war and skeptical about the value of military service. He had skills for the first time in his life, but they were useless in a society not at war. "Fit in," the Army told him. But he couldn't because he was just another whacked-out vet from a war no one wanted to remember.

He bummed around for a spell, then hid out in the mountains with Born of Songs trying to figure out what to do. Jamie and the old man tried every remedy they knew. Nothing worked. I did what I could during breaks from graduate school. That didn't work either. It went on this way for three years. Then Jonathan thought of a solution. Since the Army had trained him to be an efficient killer, he would use his skills and take to the warpath against the things that marked him Haida: Raven and Bear Mother. Kill enough grizz and ravens, he could exorcise the spirits that possessed him and force a metamorphosis that would make him a white man. He started with the grizzly on Born or Song's land. When the old man found out, he kicked Jonathan out.

For the next couple of years, Jonathan roamed Yellowstone, Glacier National Park, the North Cascades, and Alaska. Wherever there were populations of grizzly, he hired out as a bounty hunter to ranchers with bear problems. He was obsessed with making grizzlies extinct. He laced cattle and elk carcasses with strychnine, sometimes with homemade bombs with nails for shrapnel that he set off when bears came to feed. He set ambushes in garbage dumps, blew up bears with hand grenades and claymore mines he got illegally. He shot them with automatic weapons. In the winter, he blew up their dens while they hibernated. Lone bears or sows with cubs, it made no difference to him. He killed them and left them rotting where they died.

The National Park service and the US Forest Service offered a $5000 bounty for information leading to his capture and arrest, with a warning that he was armed, crazy, and dangerous. Unable to show his face in any town from the Yellowstone River to the Gulf of Alaska, he hid in the coastal mountains of British Columbia living off the land as he killed more grizzlies. But now, according to Jamie, he was back and sober.

I turned off the shower. Cold chilled over by back and chest and concentrated in my right arm around the steel pins and rods that joined my forearm to my elbow. I wiped condensation off the mirror and looked at my three-day beard. "Useless to worry now," I said to my reflection. I started to shave, energized by anticipation that filled the hollowness of my mind and body like spring water from a well.

II

Once I started talking about the war I couldn't stop. Jamie's constant questioning cracked the emotional dike I built to keep memories from consciousness. She pushed hard, and I was skeptical. Talk was useless, I told her, because only someone who went through it could understand. But occasional smiles that flickered across her lips when my stories found something funny in war's insanity changed my mind.

Her people knew the power of stories. Hearing some stories are dangerous. When you hear them, you get knowledge that kills innocence and drives you into a wilderness. You can never go back. Then like Abraham in the Bible, you either die where you are or go into the wilderness to search for a promised land that no one's ever found. That's dangerous too, only by then I figured it's better to die searching than curling up in fear under a shady rock.

I told her about the war's monotonous boredom punctuated by intense moments of violence. And how all that made it hard to sleep. You never knew when you had to be awake, so you were afraid to sleep. Sometimes, we got so tired from trying not to sleep that we couldn't remember where we were and dropped off like children. Some never woke up. Billy Joe said they were lucky because they didn't know what hit them. Jonathan said they were "fucked."

I told Jamie about how people died everyday because of small details they got too tired to deal with. Too tired to snap a flack jacket closed because it was too hot; too tired to clean a weapon; too tired to guard a light; too tired to deal with a half-inch margin of safety; just too tired to give a damn. I told her about how a talk I had with Albert Jackson the day before he died. We had just returned from a three-day patrol and were going out on another sweep the next morning. It was five minutes before I realized the film over his eyes and the dopey abstraction of his words came while he was sleeping. It was like talking to a dead man and it gave me the creeps. Albert just stood there, leaning on his M-16, responding to a dream conversation going on in his head. When I told him about it the next morning as we boarded a helicopter, he just laughed and said, "Shit, I do that all the time." He was killed twenty minutes later.

We were strapped into our seats in a Chinook on a search-and-destroy mission flying at five hundred feet. The drop zone was a group of villages north of the firebase. Just as we started to come down, something continuously hit the outside of the chopper. Across from Jonathan and me Albert tried to jump outside of his seat belt, then jerked forward and hung limp. The Chinook rose and turned sharply and slammed Albert's lifeless body back hard against his seat. A dark red spot slowly spread across the center of his fatigue jacket. It spread to his arm pits and ran down his sleeves. Jonathan unstrapped and crawled to the left door gunner, who was heaped on the floor like a cloth dummy. His hand had the bloody raw look of a piece of liver on butcher paper. Jonathan took over the gunner's .50 caliber and sprayed the ground until we got clear. We headed back to the firebase and landed fifteen minutes later, but I didn't know it until Jonathan touched my shoulder. My legs were shaking, and I couldn't stand. Jonathan thought I had been hit and pulled me off the helicopter. The Chinook took fifteen rounds. Medics scrambled to remove the dead copilot, a wounded door gunner, the dead door gunner, and Albert.

I told her about Billy Joe Johnson, a naive kid from Arkansas too friendly for his own good. He worked so hard at being likable that being around him was like being with an overeager dog. You wanted to kick him. Instead of that, everyone called him Sweet Cheeks. Billy Joe got married right out of high school and planned on going into his father's short haul trucking business before the draft got him. He never talked much about is wife because he didn't like "locker talk." He was so loyal to her he even took a vow of chastity, which to everyone's amazement, he never broke. Not even when Jonathan took him to Bangkok for some leave from the war.

But on the day he reported back from Bangkok he got a letter from his wife that blew his innocence away. She told him straight out that she was five months pregnant. Billy Joe was into the seventh month of his tour, and he was devastated. She felt so awful about it, she wrote, that she went to their church to see their minster. The minister convinced her that truth was God's way of forgiveness of sin, and she hoped Billy Joe would forgive her too. She would not tell him who the father was except that he was one of Billy Joe's friends.

Billy Joe didn't say anything after he read the letter. He just climbed on top the bunker, alone and exposed, looking toward the tree line where a VC sniper who had haunted the perimeter was hiding. His sulking kid's face was drawn up in a mean squint and a pouting smile as he stood in the open working the bolt action of his .45.

"Come down, man," I urged.

"Yeah, you'll get greased for sure," Jonathan said. "Hell, Sweet Cheeks, no woman's worth getting greased."

"If you don't get your ass under cover, I'll shoot you myself," a Private named Prager growled.

Before we could say anything else, Billy Joe cocked his .45 and rushed through the Perimeter wire towards the sniper's hole, straight up, like a runner focused on the finish line. In twenty seconds, he was fifteen feet from the hole when the sniper stood up and leveled his rifle. Billy Joe got off three quick rounds, then jumped into the hole and emptied is clip.

"That's one crazy son of a bitch," Prager said.

Billy Joe bent over the sniper's hole and worked his right arm like he was sawing wood. "What the hell is he doing now?" Jonathan asked.

"We'll know soon enough," I said. "He's heading back."

We watched Billy Joe slowly make his way through the wire. He carried something in his right hand. Thirty meters before he got back to the bunker, we saw what it was and knew not to say anything.

Billy Joe laughed and dropped the sniper's head onto a sandbag. "Best to let this cure in the sun a day or two. It'll travel better that way." Two days later he shipped the sniper's head to his girlfriend. After that, no one ever called him "Sweet Cheeks" again.

I told Jamie other stories about what happened to other men in a narrative without chronology. Some memories grated like exposed nerves, and you lash out when you can't stand them anymore, even at people you love.

She wouldn't have any of that. "You talk like a war correspondent telling other men's stories. I got that much from television and newspapers. I want to hear about what happened to you and my brother."

Well, there it was. She trapped me, and like a cornered animal, I struck hard. Not at her, but at her apartment. I threw lamps, smashed dishes, kick over two end tables, and demolished a mirror. When the apartment manager heard the ruckus and tried to calm me down, I threw him off the porch. Jamie begged the manager not to press charges, that I did a tour in Vietnam, and he sympathized. Whether that calmed me down or I ran out of gas, I don't know. But I apologized and promised to pay damages. And after we straightened out the mess, I stretched out on the couch with my head in Jamie's lap.

"The night before we got to the firebase, one of our companies—Hotel Company—was two days late from a sweep. That was the first night Jonathan and I reported in. Lots of heavy fire around the base, but no incoming. Just noise from a big fight in the hills. So next morning, several squads were sent out to make contact with Hotel Company. That was my first patrol. My squad was ordered to search around a nameless ridge, except for the number it bore on Army topography maps—986—because it was that many meters above sea level. What the maps didn't show was the way it looked to men humping through the bush that grew out of dead vegetation. So much bush, so many trees, so many hues of green that sometimes I thought I would go blind; a place where insects suck blood and chomp flesh; where snakes kill with poison so deadly it takes only two steps before life screams out of your lungs for air; where predators eat other predators and men hunt other men who hunt them."

"Sergeant Adams had a thing about Jonathan. You remember I told you he thought Jonathan would make a perfect point man because he's Indian."

"I remember," Jamie whispered.

"The fact is, Jonathan liked walking point. But he hated Adams for shoving being Indian down his throat. No one knew why Adams had it in for your brother. But you know Jonathan. He's not one to take crap from anyone. So right off he called Adams an ignorant sonofabitch. For that, Adams made him permanent point man. In fact, Adams hoped Jonathan would be killed. It really freaked Adams out when he found out Jonathan liked walking point. On our first patrol, he walked point with Albert Jackson."

"Where were you?"

"With Billy Joe and an old timer named Kruger. Kruger carried the squad's M-60 machine gun. We carried his belts of ammunition plus our own weapons. Kruger was something else. He told us he's going to blow our rookie asses away if we made any mistakes that got him wounded. See, he was rotating home in two weeks, and he would have shot anybody—us or the VC—who got in the way."

"He was serious?"

"Dead serious. I felt the same way after three months. Anyway, Jonathan and Albert were about ten yards ahead. Sometimes, we couldn't see them for all the vegetation. Finally, after hours of humping, Jonathan and Albert suddenly dropped to the ground and pointed their weapons to a pile of logs. It was good cover for a VC ambush. So, we set up a field of fire and waited for Jonathan and Albert to get closer.

"It got spooky quiet. Then I heard a bird call. It cracked the silence like the cawing laugh of a clown. The weird thing is that Jonathan and I were the only ones to see and ear it. It was perched in some trees directly over my head. A large black bird with a long yellow beak and blood red on its crown and wings. I'll never forget its amber eyes staring me down as it bobbed and weaved its head and strutted back and forth on its perch. After what seemed like a long time, it took off, circled once, shrieked, veered left, and vanished up the ridge into the bush."

"Raven must have cousins in Vietnam," Jamie said.

"That crossed my mind too, but not for long. Kruger pointed to the pile of logs. Adams and a half dozen men had worked their way behind a small outcrop of rock next to a stand of bamboo. Someone took aim with a grenade launcher and Kruger opened fire just as the grenade exploded in front of the log pile. Two more grenades exploded in the log pile. Then about thirty seconds later, Kruger ordered cease fire. I tried to spot Jonathan and Albert, but I couldn't see them for the smoke. When it cleared, I saw them moving up to the pile of logs as they signaled all clear to our lieutenant and Adams."

"I take it nobody was there," Jamie said.

"Not when we opened fire, but they had been. Charlie was one sneaky bastard."

"What do you mean?"

"Like I said, it was a perfect bunker. It overlooked a trail the lieutenant wanted us to follow. His name was Parker, and he was stupid. Everyone else knew it was sure death to walk on a trail in Nam. You could count on them being mined and booby trapped. Adams wouldn't have any of it because of that and the fact that the trail was ripped to shreds by small arms fire that we didn't lay down. Shell casings and dried blood were everywhere. Signs of a fight, but no bodies."

"Was Hotel Company ambushed?" Jamie asked.

"Didn't know for certain at the time. The old timers thought it likely. So, we moved up the ridge and kept looking. We climbed up that damned ridge for another two hours in heat and humidity so thick it was like hiking through clear glaze. Even the jungle was sweating. Somewhere near the top we stopped, and I hunkered down with Kruger and Billy Joe. Jonathan was thirty meters ahead on point with Albert checking for signs of ambush and booby traps.

"Everything went suddenly dull, as if I was looking through an opaque filter, except for the feeling I was being watched. It was that damned bird. It was perched over my head and its eyes—I'll never forget those eyes—were on me like hot rivets. I couldn't look away. Finally, it bobbed its head up and down, squawked, and took off up the ridge. I had the distinct feeling it wanted me to watch the direction it flew."

Jamie brushed her fingers over my temple, and said, "Sounds familiar. What did you do then?"

"The bird felt like a messenger, I surrendered to the feeling, concentrated on my breathing, and let lightness fill my body. Just like that time coming back from Raven's House. Only this time, I felt myself floating in the air above the summit of Hill 986. That's when I saw what happened to Hotel Company."

Jamie focused her dark brown eyes on mine. She was calm and expressionless and that surprised me. I expected some kind of reaction when I got to this part. She only asked, "What happened then?"

"I got dizzy and thought I was going to black out. So, I hunkered down stiff and tried to hold on to consciousness. The next thing I knew, Billy Joe was tugging at my arm checking me out. I asked him if he saw the bird. He just looked at me and said, 'What bird?' That's when Parker asked Adams if I was sick."

"Only you saw the bird?" Jamie asked.

"Far as I know. Adams told Parker I was OK, just doggin' it and grabbed me by my flack vest and tried to jerk me to my feet. I pushed Billy Joe away and slammed the butt of my M-16 into Adams' groin and brought the barrel down between his eyes."

"You were going to shoot him?"

"Close to it. Hell, killing him might have saved a world of trouble. Instead, I clicked off the safety and told if him to never touched me again I wouldn't give it another thought when I killed him."

"How do you figure?" she asked intensely. "If you weren't executed, sitting in a Federal prison for the rest of your life would force you to think about it a lot."

"That's another story," I laughed. "Haven't finished this one yet. Just let me get through it."

"I guess I never thought that was in you," she replied sadly.

"It's in everybody," I said. "Given the right push at the wrong time, a word spoken carelessly, or even turning away, anyone is capable of murder. The trouble is most people don't recognize it. Anyway, Adams starred cross eyed up the barrel at me, holding his groin, and threatened to send me home in a body bag. I actually started to pull the trigger when he said that. I would have too, but Kruger said don't do it and Parker was shouting at me like a crazy man. So, I backed off and told them Hotel Company was on top of the ridge about a hundred and fifty meters away. All seventy were dead, and the VC were gone. They didn't expect to hear that."

"I bet they didn't," Jamie said.

"They thought I was crazy because they didn't see the bird and there was no way to explain how I knew. And saying anything else would have been pointless. Turns out, things just explained themselves. Jonathan and Albert came running to beat hell down the hill, like men chased by something so bad they didn't dare look back or take time to be careful, as they yelled that they found Hotel Company dead."

Jamie sighed. I got up and paced around her dark living room while she sat and waited. I felt her senses key into my story and I gradually calmed down and sat beside her. "They must have smelled it before they saw them. We smelled it too after we moved closer: a sweet-and sour smell that stuck to out skins and got into our sweat. I haven't felt clean since. The summit was a flat as a Kansas prairie rectangle that sloped east to west at five degrees and pealed clean of ground cover by Hotel Company for a killing zone. There were holes all over the place, some dug by men, but most blown out by mortars. It was one hell of a fight. When we got there the only sound was the buzz of insects feasting on stripped GI corpses. The VC had stacked them in a single row of bodies ten long and five high alternating head to feet like a cord of wood."

"Jesus," Jamie whispered as I pulled her close to me.

"Billy Joe said, 'Sweet Jesus!' He always said that when anything surprised him. I couldn't find any words."

"Where there any enemy bodies?"

"None. Charlie must have carried them away. Lots of blood trails, but no bodies. Kruger said it was a message."

"A message?"

"Yeah. As Kruger put it, 'Life's a bitch and she's in heat.'"

"What then? Jamie asked.

"We set up a perimeter and called in some choppers. Then we stuffed Hotel Company into fifty body bags and the choppers airlifted them back to base camp."

"You said you saw the bodies before Jonathan and Albert. How? You weren't with them."

"That's right. Through that damned bird's eyes. When I told Jonathan, he just yelled obscenities and said I wasn't a shaman, but just another silly-assed white man. He said messing with Haida shit can get a white man killed, and I should knock it off."

"My brother's one to talk."

"That's what I told him. A Haida man trying to be white and too stupid to realize it. That just made him angrier. He grabbed me by my flight jacket and said, 'Screwing my sister doesn't make you Haida.' That made me angry, and I punched your brother in the nose. I could have happily killed him."

"I'm glad you didn't."

"There wasn't enough time. Besides, I promised you I'd bring him home. Adams, Albert, and Billy Joe broke us apart. After that, we loaded the last body bags and air lifted back to the firebase as if nothing happened. That night, all I wanted to do was sleep, but couldn't. So, I got up and went outside to get some fresh air and ran into Albert. He told me he hadn't slept much during his whole tour because he kept having the same dream. He's in a big examination room, you know, where they do autopsies. Someone hands him a questionnaire for an aptitude test. He takes it, and the first question asks, 'How many kinds of animals can you kill with your bare hands.?' He also told me about another nightmare. You know, the works—bloody stuff, bad fights, guys dying, him dying. Then he paused, shook his head, and said, 'After today, I might not dream again, and I'm scared as hell I'll miss them.'"

Jamie drew her legs under her chin and leaned against the sofa arm. "Is that when you got—what did you call it—the charm?"

"Yeah. Jonathan wouldn't talk to me for a long time, but he shot his mouth off to everyone else. It really got him when someone believed what he said. I guess they figured anyone who could see ahead of the point man just had to be venerated, though it was more hope than belief. But mission after mission, firefight after firefight, I smelled out Charlie the way hunters smell changes in the weather. They thought I had great night vision and that I had some kind of power that would bail them out of tight jams. They said I had the luck, and it would rub off on anyone who stuck with me. The thing that seemed to confirm all this was the timed I was alone in the bunker, sound asleep, when we were hit with some mortar rounds. The bunker took a direct hit and put frags through every cot but mine. That convinced them I was fast, sure, and lucky. They called it, 'extrasensory perception.' Jonathan called it, 'bullshit.'"

"What did you call it?"

"I kept my mouth shut."

12

At sundown, when the jungle gets quiet and daylight animals hole up in fear of the night, the ground seems to swell and recede. It was a peaceful feeling and I tried to relax into it and slough off the war's stress that covered me like old skin. Something always brought me out of it—a whisper, a cough, footsteps, my dreams. Then I would whisper to myself, "It don't mean nothin." Some stories are so stressful that just remembering speeds up the body's natural entropy and drains its energy like water through a sieve. Jamie's puzzled expression asked for meaning. I told her we said that about everything in Nam. I sat up and stretched my legs parallel to the floor, crossed them, and leaned back with my arms resting limply on my lap. "This last thing will take some time," I explained.

She leaned back and closed her eyes. "There's time enough," she said.

"I knew it would be bad when Major Trask started to talk like a cheerleader at a high school pep rally. The brass had a habit of sending officers like Trask to whip up morale just before they sent men out to die. 'Men,' he said, 'a force of NVA regulars is heading for An Lok. Intelligence says a full division and they're out for blood. As of now, all firebases in the area are on full alert. The fight we've looked for is here. It's the fourth quarter, and we're going to kick some commie ass.'"

"Jesus H. Christ," Billy Joe hissed under his breath. "This ain't the fucking Super Bowl."

"For certain he's never stepped in the shit," Jonathan said.

Trask paused and gazed at the men of Delta Company. Rolls of fat hung over his sidearm belt and showed he was a warrior who fought behind a desk in an air-conditioned trailer at Division Headquarters. Sweat soaked through his starched uniform and matted his light brown hair to his forehead. He looked like a mattress come to life. He had the washed-out green eyes of a dead owl. As he stood in the heat and humidity chewing on the black butt of his cigar, he reminded me of a parboiled sausage ready to burst from its skin.

"We don't know exactly where they are, so Division wants patrols day and night to probe until we make contact. We're going to catch Charlie before he gets to us. All defenses will be beefed up. When they hit, the fight will be hard."

Trask paused and squinted at Delta Company. "I know you men are spoiling for a fight. Now Charlie's heading for our turf, and this time he can't—" Engine blast from a low flying F-4 interrupted Trask's pep talk. He looked up and watched the fighter disappear into the haze. "The sound of victory," he said as he gestured to the sky, "Men, this could be the decisive battle of the war. I know you'll do your best and we'll be victorious."

"Just how many decisive battles can this stinking war have?" Billy Joe muttered in disgust. "Just once, I wish the brass would tell the truth we all know."

I slung my M-16 over my shoulder. "They don't know the truth," I said.

"Got me a bad feeling about this," Billy Joe drawled.

"Who the hell doesn't?" Jonathan growled.

When the speech was over, Trask frowned, wheeled about, and headed for the waiting Huey that would fly him to other firebases to make the same speech to other men sent out to die. We watched him lift off in a tornado of dust. Before the dust settled, the company commander, Captain Lewis, ordered all officers and squad leaders to assemble in the command bunker.

We started to break up as Adams pushed past. "Lots of good times ahead for you three. A real shit sandwich."

"Eat the sandwich and die," Jonathan hissed. "You'll be there too. Better watch your ass. Someone's likely to frag it."

I moved between Jonathan and Adams. "This bastard's life isn't worth one day in Leavenworth," I said. Billy Joe stepped behind Adams, unslung his M-16 and clicked off the safety.

Adams eyed Billy Joe and grinned. "Don't mean nothin'," he sneered. "You shit birds take it easy today." He pointed to me and Jonathan. "You two assholes have been promoted to buck sergeant and Billy Joe to corporal. Can't understand it," he said as he walked away shaking his head. "You three are as worthless as tits on boar pig. Better enjoy your promotions before someone blows your asses all over the trees."

We watched Adams disappear into the command bunker. "Well, there it is," I said.

"It's either him or us," Jonathan added. "Sure as hell, it ain't going to be us."

"If the NVA don't blow us away first," Billy Joe said. He locked and slung his weapon over his right shoulder and started to walk to the mess tent. "Let's get us a beer while we still can."

"Adams included you," Jonathan said as he fell in behind.

Billy Joe' mouth curled into a thin crescent. "Maybe so. Doesn't matter. Either Adams or the VC. I ain't coming back from this one."

He said it with such certainty that we stopped dead in our tracks. Jonathan and I looked at each other for an instant, then followed Billy Joe into the mess tent. We grabbed a couple of bottles of beer apiece, went back outside, and plopped down on three empty M-60 ammunition crates near our hootch.

Jonathan finally broke the silence. "Don't be stupid," he said. "Don't even think about it, or for sure you'll get greased." He tilted his head and drained half a bottle in one gulp. "Besides, you can't die. You have an appointment with your wife and her lover boy."

"You thick headed asshole" I snapped.

Jonathan shrugged and said softy, "Just trying to help."

Every grunt in every war has felt similar premonitions. Most were wrong, but enough were right to take seriously. But serenity glistened in Billy Joe's eyes with such strength that I knew he had seen his future without illusion, like a man with a terminal disease knows the fact of his death and accepts it. Still, I couldn't accept Billy Joe's acceptance.

"Listen to me, man," I said. "When you think of all the guys in this war, your chances of staying alive here are better than driving truck back in the world."

"Cold comfort," Billy Joe replied. He lifted is beer to his lips and drained the bottle in slow gulps. "Man, that tasted good." He threw the bottle aside and drew in a deep breath. "Never thought I drink anything except water and Cokes before I got here. This place changes a man." He reached into his fatigues and pulled out a sealed envelope and handed it to me. "This here's a letter to my wife. Mail it for me when this fight's done."

I took the envelop and glanced at Jonathan. Jonathan's eyes told me that he knew Billy Joe was a goner, except he didn't look sad, but passive and accepting of what couldn't be changed.

"I'll take care of it," I said. "But listen, man, when this thing's over I'm giving it back to you. We'll have a good laugh and get drunk."

"Thanks," Billy Joe said. "You're good friends. Best friends I ever had. Now whatever happens will be OK." His accepting smile suddenly dropped into a frown. "Just don't turn your backs on Adams. If either of you get killed, my letter might not get mailed."

There wasn't much to say after that. That's the way it was before a fight we knew was coming. No one said much of to anyone. That night I tried to sleep but couldn't. My bones felt like they were floating around in my skin. The air was heavy with human sweat and humidity, and I got the hell out of the bunker so I could breathe. It was a moonless night, but I could see the far side of a hill that defined the bowl of the firebase outlined in the orange-red glow of sunup. Flairs dropped every few minutes around the perimeter laying white light, dozens at a time tailing smoke and sparks as they hissed and lazily fell to earth. Any infiltrating NVA caught in their range would be made still, like living statues. Then the muted rush of illumination rounds fired from sixty-millimeter mortars inside the wire would drop magnesium brilliant above the statues for a few seconds outlining the gaunt spread of the trees and giving the landscape ghostly clarity before dying out. Mortar bursts would follow from three kilometers away. Then shelling from support bases further out.

I looked up at the star dotted sky above the hill's glowing and recalled what Born of Songs said about making choices. He said no one is free not to choose. What choices in a war? What a world of things to fear and choose. After I understood that I had lost fear, fear became a luxury, a trick for which there isn't any room once war's varieties of dying were accepted. Some men feared head wounds. Some dreaded sucking chest wounds or belly wounds. Everyone feared the wound of wounds. We prayed about it all the time. "Just you and me, God, right? I'll give you anything. My eyes, my legs, my fucking life. But please, don't take those." Whenever a shell landed in a group of men, the men who survived forgot about the next rounds and ripped their pants away to check, laughing with relief even though their legs were shattered or their kneecaps torn away, kept standing by their gratitude and adrenaline. And there were always choices. There were also choices no one wanted to make. Even that could be accepted. Once it was, a man could find release. There was even personal style in the way some men chose to accept their deaths.

Death could come, blood burning and crushing, as a chopper hit the ground like a dead weight. A man could fly apart in too many pieces to be stuffed into a body bag or take one neat round in the lungs and go out hearing the bubbling of his last breaths. Or he could die in the last stages of malaria with an ever-present tapping in his ears because of months of firefights. Or he could simply fall dead, and the medics would spend half an hour looking for the bullet hole that killed him while getting more and more spooked the longer they looked. He could be shot, mined, grenaded, sniped at, blown up, or blown away, so that his leavings had to be dumped in a poncho and carried to Graves Registration. Billy Joe had accepted all possible forms of dying in war. When he accepted the certainty of his own death, he felt free for the first time in his life.

I leaned against a sandbag and watched the first traces of morning cut through ground mist as the jungle began to wake up: birds calling their territory and taking wing to hunt, insects humming and buzzing, monkey sounds further out, good sounds that meant Charlie wasn't there. There was also a different bird call, a choking sound like ravens and crows sometimes make when marking their territory. It came from deep within the bush and washed over the trees like soft waves into the back of my skull. "You again," I muttered as I strained to become one with the sound. My concentration was broken by the pressure of a hand falling lightly on my shoulders.

"Shouldn't talk to yourself," Jonathan teased. "Someone might think you're nuts."

"Everyone's crazy in this country," I retorted. "Did you hear it?"

"Hear what?" Jonathan reached into his fatigues and pulled out a pack of Camels.

I nodded toward the bush. "Out there. Way out there. It sounded like a raven. I've heard that sound a lot.

"That's affirmative." Jonathan covered a match, lit up, and inhaled deeply. "Good thing, too. Our butts would be in a sling if you hadn't." He cleared his throat and spit a large mass of yellow phlegm. "Never heard it myself. The old man would say it's because Raven's your spirit-helper, not mine."

"How come you don't believe in the Haida Way?" I asked. "You were raised in it. Your grandfather's a shaman. And Jamie's as traditional as a Haida woman can get."

Jonathan laughed as he took another long drag from his cigarette. "Still don't get it, do you?" He paused and looked across the perimeter. "The trouble is, I do believe. All of it, but I don't want to." He ground his half-smoked cigarette into a sandbag. "I believe all that mumbo jumbo: talking to animals that change into human beings, spirit guides taking people into the past or the future, magic, and power. All that crap. It's real and it's crap."

"I don't understand, man."

"Simple. The Haida Way—all Indian ways—trap us on worthless pieces of land until white people think it's not worthless. Shit, you've met my grandfather. You sure as hell know my sister. Look at how they live. Used, exploited, thrown away like so much scrap."

"But still . . ."

"It ain't going to happen to me," he interrupted. "Haida spirits are real, all right. But they can't have me. I won't live my life as a Haida. Shit, I've earned the right to live like a white man in this white man's war."

I shook my head and said, "It won't work. You are who you are. Trying not to be will only get you a world of hurt."

"Look who's talking," Jonathan snickered.

"What the hell does that mean?"

"Shit, man, you know what it means. You hate being white as much as I hate being Haida."

"You don't know anything," I snapped.

"That so?" He grabbed me by my shoulders and squinted into my eyes. "Then how come it was so easy for the old man to convince you that Raven is your spirit helper? How do you explain my sister and you? She gave herself to you without a thought. They sucked you in, man, because you can't stand your own people."

I cocked my right hand into a fist and backed away. "That's bullshit."

"So, what are you going to do with that fist?" Jonathan asked.

I unclenched my fist and exhaled. "When our tour is over and we get back to the world, I'm going to kick your ass."

"You've said that before."

"I'd do it now, except I promised Jamie I'd bring you back in one piece."

Jonathan leaned back against the bunker. "You've said that before, too. What else are you going to do when our tour's over?"

I kicked the sand bagged sides of the bunker, lean back, and folded my hand across my chest. "You mean if I don't get killed."

"Never happening," Jonathan replied through a wide grin. "You've got the charm."

"Charlie and Adams might have something to say about that for both of us."

"Screw Charlie and Adams. I promised Jamie I'd bring you home."

"You promised her that?" I exclaimed.

"Sure did. I tried to tell her I could barely take care of myself, but she didn't buy it. Hell, I was drunk. What else could I do." He slapped is chest at the thought of it and laughed. "Come on, what are you going to do after the war?"

"Maybe go back to Stanford and finish up. For sure see Born of Songs. Your grandfather and I have some unfinished business, like what the hell's going on between you and your sister? Speaking of which, I intend to spend as much time with Jamie as she can stand." I watched the perimeter and tree line. "What about you?"

"Think I'll extend. I've got some unfinished business."

"Don't be stupid. Why stay in this madness when your time is done?"

"For the same reason you want to go back to Grandfather's place."

"That's not the same," I argued, "and it won't get me killed."

"Don't be too sure," Jonathan warned. "Besides, my unfinished business ain't that different from yours."

"Meaning what?" I asked. Muffled sounds of men waking up filtered from the bunker.

"Guess we'll find out when we find out," Jonathan predicted. "Sometime when both of us are back in the world."

Before I could reply, Prager and Billy Joe stumbled out of the bunker. "You two sorry-assed sons of bitches are up early," Prager said. "Let's get some chow."

"Good idea," Jonathan said. "Our conversation's about dried up. I hear the whole platoon's going out this morning."

As we slowly headed for the mess tent, Billy Joe asked, "Think we'll make contact today?"

"I expect so," I answered."

"Don't forget to mail my letter."

13

S itting by the door of the helicopter at three hundred feet, I knew we were under fire. Something tapped the Huey's underbelly like a series of ballpeen hammers, but the bullets didn't penetrate. "Sweet Jesus, the LZ's hot," a new man shouted above the roar of the rotors. We hung on as the pilot circled and came down fast as he worked the buttons that released short bursts of fire from flex guns mounted on both sides of the Huey just above its skids. Every fifth round was a tracer. The door gunners raked suppressing fire into the bush. At three feet we jumped clear and ran beneath the door gunner's covering fire through waist high grass towards the trees. At fifteen yards we dropped flat as the Huey lifted off. Both door gunners maintained suppressing fire over our heads. The rest of the company landed the same way in a line of six Hueys, one after the other. The precision of it always amazed me: men jumping into grass under M-60 covering fire, running to take positions as their helicopter lifted off and was replaced by the next. After the last Huey lifted off, the entire company fanned into a skirmish line and advanced into the jungle.

The day was hot and humid, and the sun felt like it had been dipped in lye. "Think I'll go to sleep early tonight," I panted, "and see if I wake up with any enthusiasm for this damned war."

"At least you're learning a skill," Jonathan panted. "When you get back to the world and that fancy university, you'll be one of the few who can pick off another human being at two hundred yards with a M-16."

"Not a useful skill here. Can't see fifty yards into this bush. But its definitely something to consider. A politician or two might be fun."

"Don't be bitter," Jonathan teased.

"Only crazy people aren't bitter in this God forsaken place. Like you."

"Sure as hell, it's something to do. Where the hell's Billy Joe?"

"Right behind you," Billy Joe whispered. "Y'all talk too much." He carried an M-60 and two belts of ammunition slung over his chest.

"Stay close with that weapon," I said softly. "I have a feeling this mission is going to a be long one."

After about twenty minutes of bushwhacking, the company split in two. Half headed northwest and the other half northeast. Our objective was a Montagnard village eight kilometers from the landing zone. Our mission was supposed to be simple: approach the village from two sides, scout the surrounding area for NVA, enter and secure the village, spend the night, hump back to the landing zone, and evac to the firebase and report. I was on point for the northwest column and Jonathan for the northeast column.

"See you in the village," Jonathan said. "You and Billy Joe watch yourselves.

"See you when we see you," Billy Joe answered.

* * * * * * * *

Jamie smiled, and then her expression became serious. "You've been slow getting to the meat of this story," she said. "Like a dog circling a boiling kettle of stew." She sat looking at her hands, palms up in her lap, the right hand holding the left, her fingers formed into a nest. Outside the wind whined a ghostly howl around the corners of her apartment building.

"This isn't easy," I said. "Especially knowing what to say and what to leave out."

"Don't leave anything out," she demanded. "I want to know everything."

"So I noticed," I quipped. The wind gusted and moaned louder. "The highlands in Vietnam are spooky beyond belief. Only the Montagnard live there. They didn't want anything to do with South or North Vietnam or the United States."

"But the newspapers and television news said the Montagnard were on our side."

"Army and State Department propaganda. The Vietnamese thought they were inferior, and the Montagnard didn't trust anyone but their own people. They had good reason."

"Sounds familiar. Just like my people."

"In more ways than you know. Some of them hired out as mercenaries to American Special Forces in the beginning. But their hatred of the Vietnamese eventually carried over to us."

"Were Montagnard in the village?"

"Not one."

Jamie took a deep breath. "Why was the hill country spooky? What was it like?"

I hesitated, and then said, "That's a hard one. It just felt dead, only it wasn't. The fact is, I never saw so much life concentrated in one place. That's what made it scary. Life grew in triple layers that hid the sun. Sometimes, there'd be a sudden mist that rained down from the vegetation itself. The heat of the day and the cold at night kept everyone on edge. So did the silence, even when it was broken by the thud of helicopter rotors breaking the sound barrier. The smell of the place could make man gag."

* * * * * * * *

There was movement in the trees twenty meters ahead and I dropped into a tangle of thick grass and brush. The trailing column took cover when they saw me drop. I motioned Parker, Adams, and MacDonald, who was the radio man, forward.

"What have you got?" Parker whispered.

I pointed to some trees on our left. "There's movement in those trees. There's no wind, so something's there."

Parker searched ahead with his binoculars. "Can't see a damned thing," he whispered. "Sergeant," he called to Adams.

"We're on it," Adams said before Parker could give the order. "Let's go, point man," he said to me.

We crawled ahead through the bush to the far right of the trees. Parker moved Billy Joe and three other men to covering fire positions. By the time Adams and I got close to the trees a large black bird with a red chest flushed from the trees and disappeared into the forest. On instinct, Adams rose to one knee and fired two short bursts. "Shit, it's a goddamned bird," he yelled. He looked down embarrassed, then. Glared at me. "Can't you tell the difference between a damn bird and the fucking NVA?" he said. "The VC sure as hell know were here now."

I watched the bird disappear into the forest. "I didn't pull down on the bird," I retorted, "and the NVA have known where we're going for the last two hours. They'll hit us when they're ready. Nothing will change that." I looked past Adams at Billy Joe. "They don't need to put out snipers."

"So, we waltz right through this stinking jungle," Adams sneered.

"What the hell's happening?" Parker demanded as he and MacDonald slid next to me.

"Our point man think's he knows the VC's game," Adams sneered. His face was screwed tight like a mole digging into its own darkness. "That damned bird tell you that, Elwin?"

I unlocked my M-16's safety. "You think you can do better, you sono-fabitch? Fire me and walk the point yourself."

"At ease," Parker ordered. "This war between you two ends now, or I will personally shoot both of you."

"Sir," Adams sharply responded.

"Very well," Parker said. "Elwin, get your ass back on point. We've got to make the village in two hours."

"Yes sir," I said as I moved ahead into the bush.

By 1300 hours heat trapped by vegetation got so thick it formed a ceiling underneath the trees and pressed like a damp weight on our shoulders. I reached for salt tablets and swallowed them down with a gulp of warm canteen water. I knew there would be no ambush or snipers. There never were whenever I ran into that bird. But there could be booby traps, so I stayed alert.

It wasn't long before I felt eyes tracking me. It happened before on other patrols. The first few times surprised me. But I soon came to expect it whenever I was in the bush and merely noted when it happened. The bird was perched on a limb fifty feet over my head. Its wings were folded over its back and its amber eyes looked into mine. We held each other gaze for several seconds. Then it threw back its head and cawed what sounded like a death rattle as it leaped into the air and took off toward the village. I followed its flight until it vanished. That's when I knew I would not see it again. I also knew a company strength of NVA regulars were waiting for us in the village.

We reached the rice paddies that encircled the village before Jonathan's men. So, we couched in the forest on the west side waiting for Parker to decide what to do as he swept his binoculars over the emerald rice shoots rippling in a humid southwest breeze. "You sure the NVA's here?" Parker whispered. "There's no sign of them."

Parker had been in-country for four months and the fact that he hadn't learned about the NVA amazed me. "That alone should tell you something, LT. They're here, all right."

"You see anything?" Parker asked as he passed the binoculars to Adams.

Adams scanned the village. "Wish to hell I did. The village could be a blind, but I doubt it. I've seen it lots of times. Damned VC find a village in the middle of nowhere and store all kinds of shit coming down from the north."

"A supply dump?" Parker asked.

"Affirmative," Adams snapped back.

Parker sighed. "Well, we've got to go in." He strung the binoculars around his neck and motioned to MacDonald. "Where the hell's the rest of the company? Mac, crank up that radio."

MacDonald handed Parker the receiver. "Blue Fox One, Blue Fox One," Parker whispered into the mouthpiece. "Johnson," he called softly to Billy Joe. "Set up on that knoll on the right."

Jonathan's voice cracked like a bad connection, "Blue Fox One."

"Blue Heron, where the hell are you?"

"About three clicks out," Jonathan answered.

"The village is probably a fortified supply dump," Parker said. "We're on the west side and can't tell from here. Get your people on the east side ASAP. Wait for my signal."

"Affirmative," Jonathan's voice cracked. "In thirty minutes."

"Make that fifteen," Parker ordered.

"Affirmative," Jonathan replied.

"Blue Fox out." Parker handed the receiver to MacDonald. "Stay close, Mac. We might have to call in support."

"Count on that, LT," I said. "That village is full of NVA, and they know we're here."

"How come you're so sure?" Parker demanded. "We haven't picked up any signs."

"Maybe a little bird told him," Adams quipped.

"Shut up," Parker ordered.

I ignored Adams. "LT, when was the last time I was wrong?"

"Sure hope you're wrong this time," Parker muttered.

"We both know I'm not."

"I'll be glad when this day is over," Parker said. He turned to Adams. "Sargent, form the men into a skirmish line. We go in in fifteen minutes."

Adams crawled back and signaled the men into position.

"Think I'll stay close to Billy Joe," I said. "He's got a new man tailing along, and he might need some help when things start up."

"Go ahead," Parker said. "Tell him to set up for the widest field of fire."

"He knows what to do, LT." I crawled to my left about ten yards and tapped Billy Joe on the shoulder. "We'll be going soon," I whispered. "In about fifteen minutes."

Billy Joe nodded. I dropped the clip from my M-16 and tapped it three times on Billy Joe's helmet. "Just for luck," I said as I reloaded.

"How many times you figure you've done that?" Billy Joe drawled.

I flashed an uneasy smile and looked at my watch again. "More times than I want to remember," I said. "It's worked so far."

"Not today," Billy Joe replied. "You still got my letter?"

I nodded.

"When this is over, tell Jonathan's he's one crazy sonofabitch."

"He already knows it."

Billy Joe pulled back the M-60's bolt and eased a round into the chamber. "Well, partner," his voice quivered, "good luck."

14

A teakettle hummed on the kitchen stove and a coffee pot bumped and grunted beside it. Jamie got up and went to the kitchen. "We always said that," I called after her. She came back with a mug of coffee and a cup of tea. "Said what?" she asked. She handed me the coffee as she sat next to me.

"Good luck. It was like a prayer. We chanted it all the time, but everyone gave it his own meaning. Even Jonathan. With him it always came out dry and meant he didn't care one way or the other. Adams said it too. He meant the opposite wish: I hope you die. That last day, Billy Joe said it flat to telegraph what he knew: tough shit, *sin loi*, good luck."

"What about you?"

I held my coffee in both hands and watched her sip her tea behind a light mist of steam that rose from her cup and swirled over her face. The mist pulled my attention to her eyes. By then I had come to think. That the light in her eyes could restore the sight of a blind man. They could also be as sharp as ice picks. I never tired of watching them.

"Just the passage of dead language," I answered. "There were times, though, I heard it said with such love a man's mask would crack. Like everyone else, I said it every day. To everyone in my squad, and most passionately, to myself. It was meaningless and I meant it every time."

Jamie shifted uncomfortably. "Why meaningless?"

"It was like telling someone going out in a blizzard not to get cold. It was the same as me saying, 'I hope you don't get killed or wounded or see anything that makes you crazy.' Still, it was best to make all the ritual moves because when it got down to it, the only sure thing that could be said was, 'anyone killed today is safe tomorrow.' No one ever wanted to hear that." I sat my coffee down on an end table, folded my arms across my chest and stared blankly at a rusty carpet stain between my feet.

It's funny what my mind hangs on about that day. I recall Billy Joe telling his helper—a kid named Mayhew—to stay close and keep his head down. When Parker ordered us to move out, we stepped into the paddy field. It was flooded knee deep and the stench of human fertilizer blew into out nostrils. Rice stalks moved like waves of wheat in a Kansas field, not amber but green and fertile, chest high, concealing, and beautiful. After twenty yards we spotted a large concrete bunker with slit openings low to the ground in front of a house raised on stilts. We crouched as low as we could, but Mayhew was too new not to be stupid. He stood up and said, "Oh yeah, a bunker." It was the last thing he said. All hell exploded. Automatic fire mowed down rice stalks like hail through an Iowa corn field. A red dime-sized hole imploded on Mayhew's forehead just above his left eye and exploded out the back of his skull. His head snapped back at the impact and pulled his body with it, eyes wide open, backward into the mud."

Billy Joe rolled next to Mayhew and stripped the M-60 belt from his body as he shouted that he was going to make his way to our left to get a bead on the bunker. I started to follow him, but I saw Parker hunched over MacDonald screaming for a medic. It was catching. I started to scream too: "Jonathan, where the hell are you?" over and over again as I slithered over a row of dead and wounded men bogged down in black mud like bugs on flypaper. Parker was sitting cross-legged by the time I reached him. He was holding MacDonald in his lap, rocking back and forth, screeching for medics, and telling MacDonald to hang on. I pulled Parker down and told him MacDonald was stitched across his chest. Parker kept crying and calling for a medic. I slapped him and screamed we had to move. "These aren't human beings," Parker screamed. "They're fucking animals."

The next thing I heard was a roar, like a huge rush of hot wind that sounded like a freight train just before bits of mud and hot metal exploded around us. It must have thrown me into the air and slammed me down on my right side about eight feet from Parker. There were more incoming rounds and I tried to dig a hole in the mud with my bare hands.

When it let up, I saw Parker still sitting upright in the mud staring into the sky. I reached for my weapon, but couldn't find it. So, I started to crawl back to him. That's when I knew I was hit. My right arm felt like it had been chopped off with an ax below my elbow. I checked and saw two bones sticking up like bloody ivory spikes. There was lots of blood running down my hand into the mud, and I remember thinking, "Ashes to ashes, dust to dust, blood to dirt, life to mud." I tied my arm off at the elbow and cried like a man mourning his own funeral.

Jamie moved closer and softly ran her fingers through my hair. "David," she whispered.

"It wasn't fear," I said. "Least ways, not only fear. It was something else, like a bubble that grows bigger and bigger in your gut. It puffed up against my lungs so that my breathing became short as it tore up my insides."

"I've felt that," Jamie said.

"I expect you have," I murmured as I closed my eyes. The firefight at the village was no longer a story with words hooking onto a memory, but a present reality transubstantiated in the telling.

* * * * * * * * * *

"Come on, LT, don't leave," I screamed. I took a deep breath as I turned on my left side and started pulling through the mud toward Parker. My right arm dangled like a string of sausage. "Hang on," I groaned when I reached him. Parker was catatonic. He rocked from side to side as I grabbed his flack vest with my left hand and shook hard. "Snap out of it," I yelled. "We've got get . . . oh no . . . my God, no."

Parker's head flopped to his chest. "Is it over?" Then he closed is eyes and mumbled incoherent word salad. "Is it over, Daddy? Can we go home now?"

"Your legs are gone, sir," I said as I looked for something to make into a tourniquet. It was useless. Both legs were blow off above the knees.

Parker looked for his legs. "Where did they go, Daddy?" He touched shattered bone and tissue. "Don't just sit there, Daddy," he giggled. "Find them so we can go home. We have to go home now."

"Take it easy, sir," I said as searched MacDonald's body for the radio. "Dear God, make it work," I whispered.

"It'll be dark soon, Daddy," Parker whined. "It's time to go. We can play some more tomorrow."

"We'll leave soon," I answered as I pulled the radio pack free and put the receiver to my ear and pressed the call button. "Delta 5, this is Blue Fox," I screamed. "How do you read?"

"Blue Fox, this is Delta 5," an emotionless voice cracked. "What's your sitcom?"

"Deep shit. Get me an air strike now."

"Calm down, son," the voice answered. "Follow correct procedure and give your location."

"I'm not your son and screw procedure. We're pinned down in a rice paddy in front of a village. Coordinates 8 Charlie 49. Half the company's on the east side. I don't know their situation. We're bogged down on the west side about a hundred meters from a bunker. We're taking heavy fire and mortar rounds. They're killing us. We need help now."

"On the way," the voice cracked.

"Make it fast," I said as I jammed the receiver into the pack. I pulled Parker's weapon free from his grip. "You won't be needing this," I said. Before I could tell him help was on the way, heavy caliber rounds slammed into MacDonald's body. Instinctively, I rolled over my broken arm to my left and buried my face down in the mud. It seemed like forever before the firing to stopped. When it did, there was no sound, not even the groaning of wounded men. I pulled myself up and looked towards the bunker. A line of NVA regulars streamed from the village and flanked into a skirmish line the full width of the rice paddy.

"My God," I screamed to anyone still alive, "here they come!" At their commander's signal, they pointed their AK-47s into the weaving stalks and slowly marched forward as they fired. Three men on my right stood and tried to run for the jungle. There was no footing in the mud, and they were cut down where they stood.

"Stay down," I ordered. Then I began laughing uncontrollably at the hysteria around me. I looked at Parker's dead body and said, "What the hell, LT, dead now or two minutes from now." I pulled Parker's weapon to my left shoulder and waited. "Might as well make it worth their while," I whispered to myself. And then I had another thought that worried me more than getting killed. "I hope Jamie remembers."

I set my weapon on automatic and in ten seconds emptied the thirty-round clip into the advancing NVA. I don't know if I hit anything, and it wouldn't have made a difference. The NVA line continued to advance through the paddy. Then movement ahead near the paddy caught my eye. "You son of a bitch," I cried. "You magnificent son of a bitch." It was Billy Joe. He worked his way along the paddy walls behind the NVA.

"That's it, man," I whispered. "Blow these bastards away." Billy Joe opened fire as I said it. Five NVA pitched forward, and the rest scattered for cover as Billy Joe continued to fire. "Crawl back into the jungle," I screamed.

"Billy Joe's got them pinned down." As I started to crawl away, four F-4s roared overhead, banked left, and climbed into the sun as I pulled the receiver from the radio pack.

"This is Blue Fox, this is Blue Fox."

"Blue Fox, this is Ruby Red Leader," a cheery voice with a southern accent replied. "Four birds with snake and nape. Lay in smoke and we'll do the rest."

"Negative," I screamed. "Can you see the rice paddy and the village? That's your target. Blow it to hell."

"What about your people? Friendly fire's apt to waste some of them. The NVA's awfully close."

"Just do it," I screamed into the receiver. "Everything you have. My responsibility."

"Affirmative, Blue Fox. Good luck."

I tossed the receiver aside and spotted Billy Joe just in time to see him jam a new belt of ammunition into his M-60. He resumed firing over a pile of NVA bodies. Diagonally on my right I heard the F-4s throttle down and begin their run. I focused on Billy Joe through Parker's binoculars. His expression was serene, like a man released from everything that ever made him afraid. Then the first jet dropped its load of napalm and antipersonnel mines. Fire and white heat rolled like jelly across my field of vision as the shock waves punched me unconscious.

* * * * * * * *

Jamie's eyes were hard and serious. "You told them to drop bombs on you?"

"It seemed the best thing to do at time. We were dying and I didn't want us to be the only ones doing it. The next thing I remember thinking was I was dead. Then I heard things and knew I wasn't: laughing and footsteps moving through the paddy, then nothing, then the sound of a bolt clearing an automatic weapon. I opened my eyes and squinted at dark shape blurred by backlit sunlight from a dazzling blue sky. The light was painful as I blinked against the glare as the shape spoke. 'Your ass is mine,' it said. Then it laughed again. 'I said you were going home in a body bag.'"

Jamie shook her head. "Sergeant Adams," she muttered.

"Sergeant Adams," I repeated.

"What did you do?"

"Nothing I could do. Blood was pooled in the back of my throat. I tried to stand up, but I fell back into the mud when Adams pushed the barrel of his M-16 between my eyes. That's when I knew that Adams had run out on us. I thought he got himself killed when the first mortars hit. I guess he thought I was the only witness. So, I did the only thing I could. I called him a bloody coward. He just grinned and said, 'Your Injun buddy is next.' Then he stomped on what was left of my arm and laughed again."

Tears began to pool in Jamie's eyes. "Oh David," she gasped.

"Gonna explode your head like a watermelon," Adams said.

I closed my eyes and let go of my life. "Do it," I exhaled through the pain. Waves of peacefulness overflowed my body and mind like waves at high tide as I said what I thought were my last words: "It don't mean nothing."

"*Sin loi*," Adams screamed.

"The last thing I heard was the pop of automatic rifle fire and an explosion."

Jamie looked nauseated and strange. She seemed to stand apart from her body and then merge with it. "That's the last thing you remember?" She looked astonished after she asked the question, as if she didn't mean to ask it at all.

"Until I woke up later," I answered. "It was like being wrapped in a velvet cloth, cut off from the world, even from my own body. Then I heard voices that seemed at first to come from inside my head, sort of everywhere, but nowhere."

"He looks drunk as a boiled owl," a male voice said, then laughed.

"No wonder," a husky female voice answered. "He's loaded with meds. The poor guy's lucky to be alive. You damned near killed him."

"Shit, I did him a favor," the male voice said. "He's going back to the world."

"I bet I know that male voice," Jamie said behind a faint smile.

"It sounded familiar to me at the time, too," I said. "At first, all I saw was a white glare on white walls and a fan turning slowly over my head. Two shapes came into focus, and I tried to ask them where I was. But I couldn't form the words. Pain shot through my arms, chest, and legs as I tried to cough. But the pain seemed to clear my vision and the shapes became a blond nurse and your brother. The only thing I remember about the nurse was how her hair was rolled back so tightly on the back of her head it stretched the skin of her face as tight as a drum and locked her eyes into a perpetual stare. It really threw me as she gave the IVs stuck in my arms the once over."

"She must have known what I tried to say. 'You're in a hospital at An Loc, no thanks to your friend here,' she said. Then she turned to Jonathan. 'Good vital signs. Just don't get him excited.'"

"The docs say you'll be ready to med evac to the States in a week," Jonathan said. "Drink this, man, through the straw." I raised my head, took a sip, and settled back and shut my eyes against the glare.

"How long have I been here," I asked.

"Two days," the nurse answered. "Just stay quiet and rest."

"What the hell happened? I remember getting hit . . ."

The nurse ignored me. "You explain it," the nurse said to Jonathan. "I've got rounds." She glanced at me and started to leave. "If you need anything, just call. The button's next to your pillow on the right."

We watched her leave. Then Jonathan quipped, "That's one strange-looking round eye."

"How did I get here?" I asked again. "What's she not telling me? Did they take my arm?" I tried to sit up.

Jonathan pushed me back. "She told you everything. Take it easy. You've got all your parts, no thanks to a doc at the aid station who wanted to cut your arm off. I changed his mind."

"That's a relief. How'd you do that?"

A broad grin flashed over his face. "With a cocked .45. He became a skillful surgeon real fast. They had to put your arm back together with steel."

I took a deep breath in relief and shut my eyes. "I remember Adams standing over me. The bastard was about to empty a clip into my head. Then there was an explosion, then nothing until I woke up here."

Jonathan frowned and said, "The docs said you had a bad concussion. They didn't think you'd make it. Sorry, man, it was my fault."

"What do you mean, 'your fault?'"

Jonathan pulled up a chair and sat next to the bed. "We had trouble getting to the rear of the village. When we got within a kilometer, we heard all hell break loose and ran to get to you." His voice rose with excitement. "We would have too if it wasn't for those F-4s dropping snake and nape all over the place. They almost dropped it on us."

"I remember. I called them in."

"Man, that's hard-core. I didn't know you had it in you."

"Seemed like the thing to do at the time. What happened next?"

"Well, we waited for the F-4 jocks to finish up. Then we had us a real turkey shoot. About seventy-five NVA regulars came hauling ass to get away from the napalm. We killed every last one of them."

"We were getting killed," I said. "We couldn't advance or retreat. Did Billy Joe make it?"

Jonathan shook his head. "Napalm got him. The only way we knew it was him was because of the dog tags stuck in his boots. That damned cracker was something else. His trigger finger was welded to the trigger of his M-60."

"Oh God, I killed him." I couldn't stop crying and couldn't stop whispering, "I killed him. I killed him."

"You did what you had to do," Jonathan said flatly. "It was his time. He knew it, I knew it, and so did you."

"Damn it, I've shot at people and been shot at for over seven months. And the only man I know I killed for sure was Billy Joe."

"Stow that crap," Jonathan snapped. "That was a dog-eat-dog day, and he was wearing Milk-Bone underwear. Don't beat up on yourself. The only thing the past is good for is leaving it behind."

"You should have seen him," I said. "He kept them off us until the air strike."

"He sure as hell did. There must have been over thirty bodies in his field of fire."

"Adams cut out on us and then came back after the air strike. He was about to kill me."

Jonathan shifted uneasily in his chair. "I saw him standing in the paddy pointing to the ground and laughing. That's when I tossed the grenade."

"You what? You didn't see he was standing over me about to pump my head full of lead?"

Jonathan shrugged his shoulders. "I couldn't see you. Just that bastard, Adams. I thought it was as good a time as any, so I tossed the grenade and fragged him before he fragged us." He paused and shook his head. "Would you believe he caught it like a baseball? He just looked at it until it blew the top third of him all over the paddy. But listen, man, I apologize. Shit, I'd of shot him if I had seen you."

"All I remember is Adams about to pull the trigger. How did I get here?"

"I carried you to a chopper. You were one hell of a mess. Your arm was mangled, and shrapnel was smoking from your chest and legs. The docs at the aid station thought you were too near dead to bother with, but I convinced them. Hell, you got a great wound. They're sending you home with a Bronze Star."

"Screw the Bronze Star," I said. "But thanks, man, I owe you."

"Affirmative that," Jonathan replied. "Someday, I'll collect. Besides Jamie and the old man made me promise to bring you home alive. They'd be real pissed if you got killed. I'd never hear the end of it."

"I promised her the same thing about you," I said.

"Well, it don't mean nothin' now." He stood and moved away from the bed. "I got me some R and R in Saigon." He headed out the door.

"Anyone else in the paddy make it?" I called after him.

"You're it," he said as he walked into the hall.

* * * * * * * *

A peculiar enigmatic smile glistened on Jamie's face that always puzzled me whenever I saw it. No matter how well I thought I knew her, this smile, a little quizzical, a trifle sad and filled with secret wisdom, always shut me out of her thoughts. She retreated behind this smile and asked, "What else is there?"

I put out my hand and stroked the arm of the couch as if it were the neck of a dog. "Just something Parker said two days before he died. I don't remember where he said it or why, but now it somehow glues the pieces together."

Jamie folded her hands in her lap and waited.

"He told me big companies like General Motors or Standard Oil should recruit their own private armies and fight the next war. He said no nation's army could beat it because corporations are organized to produce something for profit. It's got direction. But a nation's army is made up of millions of individuals working for themselves. Some want promotions, some want power and glory. But most want to get the hell out alive. Very few are interested in winning a war."

Jamie shook her head and frowned. "Sounds bitter and silly. It wouldn't work."

"That's the conclusion I came to after I thought about it. Human beings have the trait of murder. And besides, there's only one rule for all living things: survive. My God, the forms and species of life are armed for survival, timid for it, fierce for it, poisonous for it, intelligent for it. It's a commandment that decrees death for millions of individuals for the survival of the whole. Life's one purpose is to be alive. All the tricks and gadgets, all successes and failures, are aimed to guarantee that."

"There's still something else," she said softly.

"Yeah, I made you a promise, and I owe Jonathan Blue Heron my life."

17

Three knocks, a hesitant voice—"David?" Then a pause. "It's Jamie."

"You're here," I said as I opened the door to let her in. She stood framed like a picture, her body back lit by streetlights reflecting off black clouds of weather rolling in fast from the Pacific. Her hair was held in place by a red bandana, and she wore an unzipped parka over a Kelly-green corduroy shirt tucked inside brown wool pants that hung high over her trail boots. She carried an over-stuffed olive-green backpack in her right hand.

"Aren't you going to let me in?" she teased.

"Of course," I sputtered. "Sorry. Seeing you again has made me a bit clumsy."

She pushed past. "It's my fault you're clumsy?" she teased.

We laughed as I took her backpack and set it beside the dresser. "Are we going into the back country," I asked.

"Maybe," she replied.

"If Jonathan's in the backcountry, it'll be hard to track him."

"I'm not sure where he is." Her tone of voice said she didn't want to talk about Jonathan, and I didn't press. She pulled off her parka, tossed it on a chair, and surveyed the room. "How ugly it is," she whispered.

"There's uglier places."

"Yes, you've seen your share." She moved to me and threw her arms around my neck. I encircled her waist and drew her tight. "It will be finished soon," she whispered.

"I'm not interested in that now," I said.

She pressed her lips to mine, released me, and stepped back. "Have you eaten anything?"

I sat on the bed. "I'm not interested in eating," I said.

She moved closer and stood in front of me. "Yes, right now, we must be here in this ugly room." She reached for the back of my neck and pulled my head to her belly. My fingers were like watermelons as I fumbled at the buttons of her shirt, and we laughed out loud at my incompetence. In time her buttons relented, and I pulled open her shirt and kissed her breasts until she pushed me away and deftly undid the buttons of my shirt. When it was off, she smiled and whispered, "You're a hairless bear." Then she reached down and unbuckled my belt. I stood, and my trousers and shorts fell to my ankles. I kicked them away and went to my knees and slowly stripped her as I kissed the warmth of her thighs. Her touch signaled me to stand. She stared at me with eyes wide with delight and mischief.

I fell back on the bed and extended my right hand. She took it and raised it to her lips. For a moment there was sorrow in her eyes, and I remembered my promise. I pressed my fingers to her mouth as she set a knee on the bed and leaned down and kissed me. When I cupped her breasts her nipples hardened, and she slipped down into the crook of my arm as I turned to meet her.

We took our time. I saw that she was happy and trusting. My breathing deepened as I felt hers quicken. I rose and trailed my lips slowly from her breasts to belly to hip to thighs. She parted her legs as I knelt between them and buried my nostrils in her black tufts. She cried out in Haida as she arched her hips to my kiss. When she was ready, she took me in. The sudden sleek heat made me gasp. Her yearning scalded like hot tears as we strained and rocked in unison. Her moans became sobs, and my joy was overwhelming as I burst within her.

Afterwards, we lay in silence. Speech struggled to my lips and died. She shifted and her embrace tightened as she sighed. I kissed her lips and breasts again, slipped from within her, and rolled on my back. She scrambled to her knees and kissed my shrinking organ and pouted. "When the rabbit dies, the fox is dead," she teased.

"Be patient for twenty minutes. The fox will rise from the dead."

She kissed the scars on my chest and arm. "You've suffered much pain," she whispered.

"So have you. There's much to talk about, but not now. Come lie with me again. Time for talk will come sooner than both of us want."

She stretched out on her back. "You have become wise," she said.

Bliss surged through me again along with a realization. Love is the burning point of life. Since all life is pain, so is love. Love is the pain of being alive. I leaned over and kissed her again.

"You've found something," she said as she pulled more tightly against me.

"You're a shameless Haida woman," I teased to cover my sorrow.

"Oh, yes," she giggled to cover hers. Her hands touched my body, moved by the same interdependent forces of bliss and sorrow that human beings call love, and we abandoned ourselves to each other until dawn.

Morning came with the solitary rings of a harbor buoy swaying unevenly with outgoing tide. I heard a fishing boat sounding its horn as it passed the breakwater into the channel. Sea gulls shrieked with the horn, and I pictured them diving around the incoming boat. I imagined harbor smells: wet salt air, dead fish from the canneries, machine diesel oil, decaying piers and rusting warehouses, rusting metal, and chipping paint.

Jamie rolled next to me and kissed my forehead. "What time is it," she yawned. Her voice was velvet thick with contentment, and her breath reminded me of freshly baked bread.

"Close to five o'clock" I said.

She unwound from me, went to the window, and slightly parted the curtains. A sudden rush of gray light painted her body silver. "It's still raining," she said. "Rain clouds have covered the earth like ink wash." She let the curtain go and turned around. "Long ago, my mother told me don't ever expect a man to change. 'What you see is what get,' Mother always said." She flew to the bed and jumped into my arms. "My mother was wrong," she whispered.

"It's time," I said. "Tell me about Jonathan"

"You're right," she replied as she sat up, crossed her legs, and wrapped a blanket over her shoulder. I settled back against the headboard.

"You remember," she began, "that Jonathan drinks so much because he has dreams?"

"Of course. He said his ancestors and your people's spirits haunted him when he was sober. That was in Nam, just before our fight in the rice paddy."

"What else did he say?" she asked.

"You know perfectly well," I said impatiently. "He thought his ancestors and spirits were real. They always showed up in his dreams to haunt him because he wanted to be a white man. He was afraid they would come when he was awake, so he stayed drunk and sometimes used drugs."

She ignored my impatience and looked me in my eyes. "Grandfather sent the dreams."

"He what?" I sputtered. "That's not possible. Nam's too far away, and besides—"

"You of all people should know better," she interrupted. "Have you forgotten what Grandfather taught you? Distance and time are not problems for spirit helpers."

"You mean Raven and Bear Chief?" I asked.

She smiled. "Raven and Bear Chief," she repeated. "Grandfather even sent you a spirit helper."

"That damned bird!" I exclaimed.

"The very one," she said. "In your letters you wrote about how it got you out of a lot of tight jams."

"I'll be damned! I always wondered why no one saw it but me. Not even Jonathan. It even looked like a Raven, come to think of it, except for the red on its head and wings."

"A form of Raven," she corrected. "Raven doesn't live in Vietnam. But he can go anywhere he wants in whatever form he chooses. He was a Vietnam bird when you saw him there."

Pictures flashed on and off through my mind as fast as strobe lights: the bodies of C Company, brushes with death when I walked point, that last fight in the village. "Are you telling me Born of Songs sent Raven to Nam?"

"He didn't have to," she answered. "Raven is your spirit helper. So is Bear Mother."

I was still skeptical. "So how come Bear Mother wasn't in Nam?"

She laughed and whispered, "How do you know she wasn't?"

"I never saw anything that looked like a bear," I said.

"What about in your dreams?" she asked.

"They were mostly about you."

She leaned and pressed her lips to my right ear and whispered, "Bear Mother can be any form she wants."

I pulled away in sudden recognition. "Bear Mother's your spirit helper," I blurted. "Her form was you?"

"Something like that. Grandfather wanted to convince Jonathan he was on a foolish path. He also wanted to protect you, so he sent Raven. I didn't want you hurt or killed either. So—how can I say it?—I dreamed your dreams. You were never alone."

"Except for that fight in the village," I said. "Guess that's why you never answered my letters." There were more flashes of memories: Albert Jackson dangling from a safety belt in a helicopter bleeding to death from a sucking chest wound; Billy Joe Johnson holding off advancing NVA until he was blown apart by friendly fire; Sergeant Adams standing over me; Jonathan saving my life. "Lots of men could have used that help," I whispered.

"You must not feel guilt for the death of your friends," she replied. "Life and death are gifts, and every gift has a price."

"And now it's time to pay up," I said.

"For both of us," she said.

"That's why I came to Ketchikan to meet you. Tell me what's going on."

Daylight approached like a thief as the first rays of dawn lit a gray corona around the edges of the red window drapes. Jamie shivered and tugged the blanket around her shoulders. "Jonathan showed up at the cabin three weeks ago," she began. "He was sober as a judge and crazy excited about an idea he said came to him in the back country after he ran out of whisky."

"What idea?" I interrupted.

"How to stop dreaming. How to change from a Haida man into a white man. He said he had been going about it all wrong when he killed all those grizz. He said all he had to do was kill Bear Chief and Bear Mother."

"Your people's ancestors?" I blurted. "That's crazy. Myths are hard to kill."

"The ancestors are as real as we are," Jamie said. "You've even met Bear Mother."

"Hell, that was just a pot-induced nightmare."

"Before that, on the trail to Raven's house when I took you there for the first time."

I swallowed hard. "I don't believe this," I protested.

"I know it's hard to believe, much less understand, even for my people. But listen, David, you've lived in two worlds since that time at Raven's House. You must understand what you know, not what you believe."

"Right now, I'm not sure who's insane, Jonathan or me." I swung my legs over the side of the bed and sat with my elbows resting on my knees.

"I know it's hard," Jamie said. "Just listen to the rest of it." She moved close and gently stroked my neck and shoulders. "Bear Chief is the biggest of all grizzly bears, and very old. I've never seen him, but Grandfather has. He lives with Grandfather on the land around Raven's house."

"And Bear Mother is your helper spirit," I said flatly.

She rested her head on my shoulders. "Yes, my love," she whispered into my ear. "But she's more like a relative. Every Haida in my clan is descended from her and Bear Chief. Even you because Grandfather adopted you. Without them, there is no Bear Clan. That's what Jonathan figured out."

"You mean he thinks if he kills them, he won't be Haida and actually turn into a white man?"

"That's about it," she replied sadly. "He's like a child about to murder his parents. And if he succeeds, the Bear People will die too. Jonathan, Grandfather, you and I, the whole Bear Clan will die. Rubbed out, as if we never existed."

I had never seen such fear in Jamie's eyes. "Let me get this straight," I said. "You're telling me if Jonathan succeeds in this, the Bear Clan will become extinct, like the Last of the Mohicans?"

Jamie shook her head. "Not extinct. The Bear Clan, including you and me, Grandfather, and Jonathan, will have never lived."

What she meant finally sunk in, even though I didn't believe it—at least completely. Hell, I still don't believe it. Now I know. But at the time, I just said the next thing that popped into my head. "So, you want me to stop Jonathan from killing these two grizz. Why? I mean if they're what you say they are, they don't need my help. It seems to me that Jonathan's the one in trouble, not Bear Chief and Bear Mother. Besides, why doesn't your grandfather put a stop to this nonsense? He's a shaman and should have the power to stop Jonathan."

"You're right," she snapped. "Jonathan's the one in danger. If you track him down, it won't help Bear Chief and Bear Mother. It's for Jonathan's sake. Stopping his foolishness will save his life. Besides, Grandfather is too old. This is why Raven and Bear Chief have given you power."

"Hell, Jamie," I protested. "I'm not Haida and I'm sure not a shaman. What power are you talking about? You say I'm adopted, but I'm still a white man and your ancestors are not mine."

"Come on, David! Admit what you know. You are a white man and a Haida man. Loose your fear and follow your vision and live in your white world and the Haida world. If you don't make your mind as large as the universe so there's room for paradox, Jonathan will die, and we will live in two different worlds."

There it was. I watched two lines of tears trickle from her eyes down both cheeks. "Our people," I muttered. "So, we can't be together unless I do this thing." I buried my face in her long hair and whispered, "Jonathan may die anyway. He's nuttier than a truckload of pralines. It may be the only way to stop him is to kill him. Are you and Born of Songs ready to pay that price?"

"Are you his best friend?" she asked.

"I honestly don't know. I've had enough of killing. And besides, your brother would be hard to kill if it comes to that. Lots of men have tried. I'd rather talk sense into him."

"That will be harder than sneaking moonrise past a cayote," she answered. "He's determined to kill everything that makes him who he is. Or anyone who tries to stop him, including Grandather and me."

"Or me, if I agree to take this on." I added. The familiar anxiety of combat rose, like low voltage electricity, from my belly and flowed into my arms and legs. I locked my arms around her as day sounds grew louder. Jamie looked with disappointment at the dim sunlight filtering around the curtained window.

"Another day has turned on," she said wearily, "like a switch."

I stood and pulled my trousers from the chair and started to dress. "Where are Jonathan and Born of Songs now?" I asked.

"The last time I saw them together was at the cabin. Grandfather went to Raven's house a week ago. He said he couldn't stand being with Jonathan. He was also in a hurry to finish a new totem pole." She stood up and walked into the bathroom.

"Seems strange that he's carving a new pole. What kind of pole?"

"I don't know," she answered as she turned on the shower. "What now?"

"Talk to Born of Songs and Jonathan."

16

F og hung like soaked gauze over the black-green forest where we turned off onto the mud road that dead ended two hours later at Nathan Born of Songs's cabin. The first four miles ran straight toward the small foothills of the mountains. The forest had been logged off long ago, and now green grass gave the foothills a wet bloom of young summer. It's a rare day when it's not raining in this part of the Alaskan Canadian wilderness, and the land seemed intent in showing its most somber tones. Jamie and I didn't speak. There wasn't any need. I concentrated on keeping my pickup on the road and Jamie stared straight ahead. He body bounced hard against the seat belts as she stiff armed the dashboard to brace herself.

I dropped my pickup into fourth gear. Birds flushed out by the transmission's whine flew out of the ground fog and sought cover up in the trees. Huge rocks broke through the ground like ancient tomb stones, testimony to thousands of years of life carved by an eternity of rain, and velvet-green moss covered the stumps of logged off trees and the cedar shingles of occasional cabins. It was dark by the time we saw the lights of Born of Song's cabin. By then the road had transmuted into a dirt road passing between two groves of red alders before it butted into Born of Songs's front door. Overhanging branches scraped the top of the cab as we pulled in beside an old pickup with a rusted silver cover over its bed. I shut down the engine and listened to the wind blowing through the trees.

"Is that Jonathan's rig?" I asked.

"He's lived in it for two years," Jamie answered.

I opened the door and stepped out. Sudden movement at the forest's edge on my right caught my eye, and I dropped to my knees and reached under the driver's seat for my .45 pistol.

"What is it?" Jamie asked anxiously. "Are you OK?"

I cursed under my breath. "Old habits die hard."

"You saw something?"

I pointed toward the forest. "Movement over there, and now footsteps."

By then it was dark, but not dark enough to hide the shadow not worrying about being seen walking toward us. As the shadow got closer, it called out, "Is that you, man? This isn't a fit place. Only a couple more days."

"Good to see you too," I answered. "It's been a while."

Jonathan took off his hat and shook off the water. His hair was tied in a single braid and interwoven with black raven feathers. A necklace of canine bear teeth hung around his neck. "Rather see you in Seattle or Ketchikan." His voice had a curious edge.

"Sure," I replied. "But since we're here, we might as well go inside and get warm."

"How's Grandfather?" Jamie asked sharply.

"Don't worry, Sis," Jonathan answered as he started walking toward the cabin. "He's doing his thing and carving another totem pole. Claims it'll be his last."

I tried to change the subject. "You know, it's been a long time since we've been together without someone trying to kill us. It seems odd."

We went inside. Jonathan flopped on the couch, head thrown back, and legs spread wide toward the crackling cedar burning in the fireplace. I pulled off my jacket and threw it over a chair.

"Your war's over, man," Jonathan said. "Best not look for another one."

Jamie slammed the door shut, went to the table, and pulled out a chair and sat. "Maybe you should take your own advice," she said to Jonathan.

Jonathan glanced at Jamie and then fixed is gaze on me again. He eyes seemed tired and as vacant of life as the open eyes of a corpse, then suddenly came to life again. "Hell," he laughed, "the only thing I know is war. Oh, I sometimes think I know all sorts of things, but all I really know is the warpath.

"I hear you, man," I said. Then we got hysterical with laughter. We laughed when we looked at Jamie staring at us. We giggled and chortled and yelped like teenaged boys telling dirty jokes, except we told war stories. I started with the time a rookie on a mortar crew in his first firefight set the elevation wrong and the round came down on the officer's latrine.

"Yeah, talk about being scared shitless," Jonathan wheezed.

We slapped our knees and banged our fists on the arms of the couch. Tears came with laughter, and we hugged each other to steady ourselves and not fall faint as our laughter wound down.

"Maybe it's the rain," Jonathan chuckled. "Sometimes, you've got to laugh or kill something." He let go of me and wiped his eyes with the heal of his right hand. "I'm a fucking clod, man, just like Billie Joe. All those VC I killed. All those grizz. They're coming for me."

"The Vietnamese have lots of relatives," I said. "Don't worry about dead Vietnamese, just their relatives. Never go back to Vietnam, that's all." I pointed to his braid and necklace. "And leave the grizz and ravens alone. You'll be all right."

"You noticed," he said proudly as he lifted the necklace. "The canine teeth of every grizz I killed, from Montana to Wyoming, to Alaska. I've got over two hundred teeth here."

"And the raven feathers?" I asked.

"The tricky little bastards are hard to do." He let the necklace fall back to his chest. "Now they'll know it's me who's killing them."

"They've always known," Jamie interjected.

Jonathan was wrapped too tightly in his mind to hear her. "When it's over, I'll toss the necklace in the bush, cut off my hair, and . . ." He suddenly sat up and changed the subject. "When I was in Nam, after you went back to the world, when you were in school and balling my sister and getting soft, I met a white grunt who took scalps. I didn't go for that myself."

"Keep talking like that," I warned, "you'll find out I'm not as soft as you think." I shifted my weight and asked, "What was your thing?"

He suddenly stiffened, then relaxed, and flashed a sly grin.

"What are you thinking about now?" I asked.

"Do you remember when Billy Joe went crazy and killed the sniper?"

"Yeah, so?"

"How he cut off the snipers head and mailed it to his wife?"

"Sure, get on with it," I said impatiently. I glanced at Jamie. She was frowning and I thought, "Well, my love, you wanted to know it all."

"I mailed VC ears to officers," Jonathan boasted. "Company commanders, battalion and division commanders, CIA spooks, hell, even chaplains." He paused and thought for a moment, then continued, "Never found out if Slippery Dick Nixon or Westmoreland's wife got theirs."

It was disgusting. Still, any grunt who served in Nam would have wondered at the sheer ambiance of it. "You are one crazy sonofabitch," I said. "Magnificent and nuts. You're so scary you'd turn a funeral up an ally."

"Hear that, Sis?" Jonathan said to Jamie. "Your boyfriend talks to birds and thinks I'm crazy?"

"Enough, Brother," Jamie ordered angrily. "David's our guest and friend. Treat him the Haida Way, with respect."

Jonathan jumped to is feet and started toward Jamie. "Don't tell me what to do, bitch," he screamed.

I jumped in front of Jonathan. "Back off," I warned. "This isn't the time or place."

Jamie stood and confronted her brother's rage with her own. "Brother, you are in my circle of power," she warned. Her eyes lashed through narrow slits, and I knew she could—and would—send Jonathan straight to the spirit world with a wave of her hand. Jonathan knew it too and backed off.

"Come on, man," I pleaded. "Tell me what's happening. Maybe I can help."

"Shut the fuck up," Jonathan snapped. He continued to watch Jamie stand her ground. "Don't need any help. I've got everything figured. In two or three days, it'll be over."

"Don't do it!" Jamie both implored and warned. "If you pull it off, our people will die. So will you."

"Everything dies sooner or later," Jonathan whispered. "Hell, our people have been dead for a hundred years."

I thrust my hand past Jonathan against the door and stiffed armed it. "Give it up, man. There's no life in killing. You should know that by now. We've seen too much death. End it, here and now, while you can."

"She's told you what I'm gonna do," he said as he pushed my hand from the door. "Did she say why?"

"Yeah, she did."

Jonathan pushed open the door, paused, and asked, "Do you believe her?"

Cold damp air pushed in by a passing squall whipped into the cabin. "She's never lied to me," I said.

"Neither have I," Jonathan retorted. "So, you best believe this. I will kill the Chief Grizz and Sow Grizz in these mountains." He nodded to Jamie. "If you, or anyone else try to stop me, I'll kill the both of you, too."

I stepped back and said, "Well, there it is."

"There it is," he repeated in an emotionless flat voice. That's when I knew my best friend was on a path from which he could not be turned. "You've been living fat since you got back from Nam," he whispered. "Don't let down."

* * * * * * * *

When the night sky over Raven's house fell black and high mist dulled the sharpness of the stars and muffled forest noises, Born of Songs set down his tools and studied the totem pole in the light of a campfire. It was the largest pole he had ever carved, standing over forty feet high. He also knew it would be his last. For months, he carved his vision of the story of the people. Now the pole was finished, except for the top figure. He could not find it in the wood. It wasn't time yet, and he hoped that Raven's cousin, Owl, would not call his name before he found it.

When he put out the campfire and went inside Raven's house, he felt his way through the interior darkness to the fire circle. He marveled how heavy his body felt with age, and dampness chilled him to the bone. He crouched and groped for the wood pile he kept stacked near the fire circle as he reached inside his flannel shirt for matches. He found one and scratched it across a stone. The match exploded into a flicker, and the sudden light seemed to surprise the darkness. He cupped the match with his hands and carefully lit the dry shavings under the larger pieces of wood. As soon as he felt the fire's heat spread up his arms and across his chest, he moved back, stretched out on an elk hide, and drew a bear robe over his body.

Thoughts and emotions bubbled into his mind as if from an ancient spring. How when he was very young he knew that the earth was full ghosts, and his father said, "No, that wasn't right. Ghosts are weak shadows of reality. What lives on the land is more than we. It's we who are like ghosts of their reality." He remembered how his mother taught him that the earth is everything's mother. Now he wondered how soon he would be going back to Mother Earth.

He studied the red coals of the fire as he thought, trying to divine the future. He listened to the crackling sounds of the fire, and while his eyes did not move, there was an air of attentiveness in them. Gradually, at the end of the day, when night's darkness comes as imperceptibly as age comes to an old man, Born of Songs put the top figure he would carve into the sacred red cedar log into his mind.

"Raven," he called into the darkness. "There's so little time. That's the only thing that makes me sad."

"Why are you sad, Old Man? Everything is going as it should."

"Because when a man lives long enough with you, there's not much under the sky that can make him sad. Except the passing of time."

"Have you already forgotten everything I taught you all these years, Old Man?"

"I remember. I also remember when I was young, without experience and full of juice, a day had twenty-four hours. Days are shorter now."

"A day still has twenty-four hours."

"Yet each day feels shorter than the last. Each day winds down to the split second of my passing from life to death."

"That makes you afraid? Where is your wisdom?"

"I do not fear my death. It is the order of things, and not to be feared. But death is not to be rushed into, as my grandson does. No, Raven, my old friend, I only fear not having enough time to finish this pole before you send Cousin Owl to call my name."

"I haven't decided when your time comes. Are you wiser than me?

"No, Raven. But I hear it in the wind and sleet pounding on this house. My life is running headlong into the formless flow of time itself, like water running off the land after a cloud burst."

"Your grandson is on a blood trail now. Is that what you fear? Don't worry, I've taken care of everything."

"My power gets weaker every day, but I still know that much. I also know David and my granddaughter were at the cabin with Jonathan. Jonathan will begin his hunt tonight. David and Jamie will come here in the morning."

"You still see well, Old Man. Does not what you see please you?"

"How they will pass the night makes me feel young again."

"Is that all?"

"No, old friend, there's more. You know what it is. My granddaughter will give David knowledge to hear the voices of stones and trees that sing music. Then David will not live like other white men."

"Or like other Haida, Old Man. Don't forget that."

"Because hearing the songs of stones and trees, and animals will lead him to the songs within himself. He will inhale the breath of the Unseen."

"It will be harder for him than it was for you, when I first moved you to the song of life."

"The white people call this knowledge 'supernatural.' At first it will seem so to David, as it was when you and my father first passed it on to me. My granddaughter, Bear Mother's Daughter, will teach him it is of nature itself."

"She has already started."

"Yes, old friend, David will take my place and all will be well."

"Then why does sorrow weigh on your heart like a stone."

"It is the path I once hoped my grandson would walk."

* * * * * * * *

Jamie and I watched Jonathan disappear into rain sheeting down and splashing on pools near the cabin's steps. The slosh of his footsteps abruptly stopped, and we heard Jonathan's pickup door squeak open, and slam shut. "I wonder why he's in the truck," I said. "There's nowhere to drive, except down the hill. Does he sleep in it?"

"As far as I know," Jamie replied. "Least ways not since he came back three weeks ago. But I don think he sleeps all that much, if at all."

I shut and bolted the door. "Best to keep him out. A man who doesn't sleep is afraid of his dreams."

"And of himself," she added as she sat on the floor in front of the fireplace.

I moved beside her. "Dangerous, but not totally unpredictable. At least we know what he's made up his mind to do."

She nodded. "He will start out early in the morning, before daylight," she said sadly. "He has set his path."

"There's only one choice now," I said as rain began to pound harder on the cabin's roof. I took a deep breath and exhaled. "I hoped it wouldn't come to this. Hell, I might not be able to do it."

Jamie stood up and walked toward the bedroom. "We'd better get some sleep," she said. When she returned with an armload of blankets, I helped her spread them on the floor in front of the fireplace. "The first thing we do is find Born of Songs," I said. "I might need something extra." I sat and began to remove my boots.

Jamie stood over me and started to undress. "You mean *we* might need something extra," she corrected. "No way you're leaving me behind." She wrapped herself in a blanket and sat next to me. "Do you have a plan?" she asked.

"No, and I'd rather do this alone. You'll just be in the way. If you tag along, I'll worry about you and that will slow me down. It could also get us both killed." As I finished undressing, she opened her blanket and I folded myself into her warmth.

"I'm coming with you," she asserted. "I brought you into this. So did Grandfather. We'll finish it together."

I knew I couldn't stop her. I wondered if I really wanted to. She stretched out across my lap and looked up into my eyes. "I love you," I said, and knew this time it was an announcement of fact instead of a plea.

"I surely love you," she answered in a voice sweet and hopeful as a tired sigh.

"I guess I've known it all along, even though you never said the words."

"It's better to show it than to say it."

"But you say it now," I said softly.

She smiled as her eyes became moist. "It's necessary now," she whispered. "The words are power words." She lifted her head and kissed me. "On our first night here, I wondered how I could make the night last. I tried to hold to it until I got another as good."

"Love, like death, is an ultimate mystery," I whispered. "It's sad to miss one when the other is inevitable."

She slid beside me as I laid back and rested my right hand on her thigh. She stretched her legs and moved closer as my body tightened in anticipation. Then she whispered an afterthought: "There are times when love is strong and warm—like sorrow."

17

Jonathan Blue Heron's life was full of spirits, and they closed in on him like stalking wolves. He wondered why they were so hungry for food and sex, for sunlight and being warm, for family and laughing with friends, for everything that makes life alive. They starved for Jonathan Blue Heron's life, and they wanted to make him one of them. When they did, they would still be hungry. Jonathan sat with his spirits in the pickup and watched the cabin's windows. "She had to bring him here," he muttered to himself. "She and the old man can't stop me. They know David is the only one who can."

He reached for a large backpack on the floor in front of the passenger seat. "Time for an equipment check," he whispered. "Let's see . . . ten clips for the M-16, fifty rounds for the .45, four hand grenades, and this little beauty." He held up a claymore mine and smiled. "Had a hard time stealing this," he chuckled. He listened to the rain pounding the pickup as he strapped the .45 on his right hip. As he climbed out of the pickup, he listened to the wind moaning through the trees and it reminded him of a woman in labor. "It's sad when a man hates his life and can't deal with it," he said to the wind. "He must fight against killing the people he loves."

He looked back at the cabin's windows and saw a shadow slightly darker than the darkness that outlined it. "I'll kill this man who is my friend," he promised the wind. He watched the shadow melt into darkness, slung his backpack and M-16 over his shoulders, and walked into the forest. "Those two are in for a real interesting time," he cheerfully said to his spirits. "You're about to see a real pro at work."

* * * * * * *

David woke at dawn and wrapped in a blanket went to the window. Clouds rolled west to east like a curtain of gray wool as dawn began to sparkle on the washed land. The western range was edged in silver, but the valley below the cabin was still filled to the mountain rims with night. Overhead, in the steel gray fabric of the sky stars seemed to struggle and wink against the approaching daylight. An invisible northbound squadron of Canada geese honked plaintively, and a great horned owl hooted the last night's hunting. The wind brought fir smell and the bouquet of vanilla plants mixed with the odor of a skunk's anger, smelling, since it was so far away, like azaleas.

He heard Jamie stretch out against her blankets. "Is Jonathan still in the truck?" she asked in a voice husky with sleep.

David glanced at the faded green-and-rusting three-quarter-ton pickup with dents in both front fenders and spotted with gray primer. "He took off on foot a couple of hours ago. Leastways, that's when I heard his footsteps disappear into the brush. From the sound of it, he was heading north and packing a lot of gear."

"We'd better get on his trail," Jamie said excitedly. She reached for her clothes and started to dress.

"There's still time," David said as he turned from the window. "I need to pack some things."

"What kind of things?"

"Oh, the usual stuff. Sleeping bags, a tent, rain gear, food. My guess for about three days."

"What else?" She stomped her right foot into a boot and began to lace it tight."

"My Winchester, a Colt .45, and enough ammunition."

She pulled on her left boot. "Don't worry about bringing food." She stood and went to the stove, struck a match, and set it to the wood and paper in the firebox. "It's best to travel light. We'll eat a good breakfast here and live of the land. But I left my sleeping bag and rain gear in Ketchikan."

"Everything we need is in my truck," David said.

"Maybe Jonathan took it to keep us from tracking him."

David felt her nervus energy as she began preparing their breakfast. "That's not likely," he said. "Your brother wants us to go after him."

"But I thought—"

"Slow down," David interrupted. "Your brother's a trained hunter and tracker. We'll need to conserve energy and keep focused to catch him."

Jamie slammed the iron coffee pot against the stove. "Damn it, he's got a big start," she shouted."

"Calm down," I ordered. "Jonathan was right. Your power isn't out there. Settle down, and I mean now, or I'll leave you here and go after Jonathan alone. You'll be less than useless out there if you don't get control of yourself."

She turned and faced me as her eyes blazed and her body stiffened. And then just as suddenly, she relaxed and whispered, "You're right. I'm so sorry." Then she brushed her right hand across her forehead and turned back to her cooking.

"I'd rather have you with me," I said. "You know this country."

She set the coffee pot on to boil. "What now?"

"First, we eat. Then we hightail it to your grandfather. I've got a hunch he's expecting us."

* * * * * * * *

It was close to noon and Nathan Born of Songs sat on an old stump watching where the trail from his cabin broke through the trees onto the small clearing surrounding Raven's House. He had sat there since the night started to edge toward dawn when trees and grasses whisper their messages through a fresh morning breeze. "So, you have come," he called out.

"It's been a long time, Nathan Born of Songs," I answered. I dropped my backpack and rifle. "But you've been on my mind. Are you well, Old Man?"

"Well enough," he answered. He glanced at Jamie and smiled. "But my power seeks to live elsewhere. Soon, I must leave this world."

"But not before you finish the pole, Grandfather," Jamie said.

Born of Songs chuckled. "That's not for me to decide, Granddaughter. Maybe Owl will not call me before it's finished. Who knows? And you, my son," Born of Songs said to me. "Are you well?"

"Well enough," I answered. "Better if Jonathan snaps out of it."

"My grandson is beyond hope. Now it's up to the ancestors."

"That's why I came," I said. "What have they decided?"

"I don't know," Born of Songs answered sadly. "I am losing my power. They have not told me; except we can't help him."

I picked up my backpack and rifle. "Still, we must try," I said. "The three of us." I motioned to Raven's House. "First, we must talk. When that's done, Jamie and I will track down Jonathan.

Nathan Born of Songs raised his right hand. "This is man's work," he protested.

"We've talked about that," I said. "I don't like it either, but she's made up her mind. Besides, she knows these mountains and where Jonathan is likely to go."

"Don't you know he will kill anyone who comes after him?" Born of Songs asked. "You will have to kill him. Are you ready for that, my son?"

"I hope it won't come to that. It won't be easy if it does. Your grandson is highly skilled."

"Answer straight," Born of Songs demanded. "Can you kill your friend?"

"My best friend," I said as I looked away at the unfinished totem pole. "I owe him my life. Still, there are times when something awful—something old and powerful—takes a man over. When that happens, it's best to kill him and get it done, even if you love him."

"And you, my granddaughter," Born of Songs asked Jamie in a voice that seemed to blend with the wind blowing through the fir trees. "What does Bear Mother's Daughter say?"

"Bear Mother's Daughter says her brother is crazy," she answered. She focused her cold gaze into the old man's eyes, as to confirm her intention into Born of Song's mind. Then she spoke as if to seal in his memory what she expressed through her eyes.

"I love my brother as I love our people. But his life is controlled by bad spirits he made himself. They will take his life even if we stop him from killing Bear Chief and Bear Mother." She turned and pointed north toward a saddle backed ridge of mountains. "We must get there before he does. If this means my brother must die, at least he will be with our ancestors. He'll be better off than he is now."

With that, Born of Songs turned and walked briskly into Raven's House. We followed in silence, and when we reached the fire circle we sat in our usual places: Born of Songs on his elk hide, Jamie under the outstretched paws of the grizzly hide, and me directly across from her. Born of Songs leaned over the coals smoldering in the fire circle and arranged some fresh wood. He gently blew on the coals until the wood ignited. Then he sat back and broke the silence.

"It won't be easy, and I can't go with you. I would slow you down." He spoke like a man rehashing a conclusion he didn't like. "Life cannot be cut off so quickly," he said. "No one is truly dead until the things they changed are dead. As long as someone remembers my grandson, even if the memories are bad, he cannot be cut off, dead."

"This isn't time for Haida mysticism," I said with some irritation. "All I know is what I've seen. All people die, some quick and some slow. I killed some of these people in Nam. So did Jonathan, probably more than he can count. I tell you the things of their lives made no difference to them or to us. They died and became worthless. American or Vietnamese, white or black, all the same. Jonathan never gave their death or his a thought. That's his edge."

"Why's that an edge?" Jamie asked.

"Because a man like Jonathan will inflect a great deal of death without a single thought."

Born of Songs spit into the fire. "That makes my grandson weak," he said in disgust. "That's your edge."

"How's that?" I asked.

Born of Songs reached to his left for a piece of cedar and tossed it into the fire. "A crazy man is never afraid, so he can never learn about courage. That's your edge. You have not turned your back on death. You've faced it head on and found courage."

"That remains to be seen," I said. "The question is still what to do if we find him."

Born of Songs nodded at Jamie. "You've talked this over and decided. But it is a man's hunt. It's too dangerous for—"

Jamie broke in. "David must not do this thing for us, but with us. I am Bear Mother's Daughter, and you are Raven's son. Our clan, the Bear People, have adopted this white man to help us do what we must do. It is decided. I will go with David."

"When we find him," I said, "he will give us no choice. I don't want to kill my friend. The fact is it will come to this. One of us, Jonathan, or me—or maybe Jonathan or you and me—might be killed."

Jamie folded her arms across her chest and gazed into the fire. Born of Songs closed is eyes and sat motionless, like a Buddhist monk I once saw in a Vietnamese village sitting peacefully in meditation while blocking out the war's external violence from the inner journeying of his mind. Outside, the shriek of an eagle broke the silence. "Remember," Born of Songs cautioned, "a warrior always leaves his enemy one chance to escape. If he refuses to take it, he has killed himself."

18

It is a defining trait of the human spirit that truth can be known and not accepted. Jonathan was heading to his death. This knowledge came during the night from Born of Songs. Everything, he told us, was out of our hands. "Jonathan is too far gone," he said. "The ancestors are tired of him, and his path is decided. You will be witnesses, nothing more."

"Still, we must try," I replied. "He once kept a man from killing me. I must try to keep the ancestors from killing him. I owe him that much. He is my friend. It's as simple as that. Jamie is his sister. Also, as simple as that."

So, Jamie and I left Raven's House the next morning, just as the day's sunlight caught the top of the trees and began hanging over the land, changing colors but never fading. At the foot of the last steep pull to Raven's House, where the trail abruptly bowed left and switch backed down the hill for a quarter of a mile, we heard the creek. Jamie led the way from the trail's cut off.

"Lord, how the day passes," I said as I looked up at a patch of blue sky. "Just like life. Fast is you don't watch it and fast if you do."

"White people's time," Jamie puffed. "My people think the future is slow. It's the past that's awful fast." She stopped and pointed north. "The creek's down that way, about a mile or so. We'll follow it until it curves northwest. Then we head straight up that mountain. There's a big cave halfway up. My people say that's where Bear Chief and Bear Mother live."

Old instincts began to cover in my body as I unslung my Winchester, checked the load, and made sure the safety was locked. "Is that where we find Jonathan?" I asked.

"That's where we find him," she answered.

I unbuckled my .45. "Better take this," I said. "See, all you have to do is take off the safety by pushing this lever forward with your thumb. Then pull the chamber back and let go. One round in the chamber and seven in the clip. Then all you have to do is point and squeeze the trigger."

She stepped back as she said, "I hate guns. I don't want it."

"I hate guns, too," I said. "Take it anyway. It will make me feel easier. Besides, you may have to cover my backside." I aimed the pistol at a tree with both hands. "Just hold it this way," I instructed. "Sight down the barrel and squeeze the trigger. Remember, it'll kick hard to the right."

After I reset the safety, she took the gun belt and strapped her right hip. "If it makes you happy," she muttered under her breath.

"It does," I said.

"But I won't shoot anything."

"You won't know that until the time comes. Nobody does. So, if I can't count on you, go back to Raven's House."

I wasn't sure she could fire the .45 if it came to it. Killing isn't in her nature. But in Nam I learned never to be caught in the bush with someone I wasn't sure about. I could have made her go back, except Jonathan might circle back and Jamie might walk into him. There was no choice.

"I'll take the lead," I said as I started toward the creek.

"You don't know the way," Jamie protested. "There's no trail from here on."

"You have no experience with this sort of thing. It's best that I walk point. Jonathan has probably set some traps and you don't know what to look for. Stay five yards behind but keep me in sight and keep me headed in the right direction. From now on do exactly what I say and when I say it. No questions. Just do it."

Jamie nodded affirmatively and said, "I hope this weather holds. I'm tired of being wet and cold all the time."

"Maybe it will," I replied. "But no more talk now. Whisper only when necessary. Now, let's get this done."

As soon as we stepped off the trail, the tops of old growth Douglas firs blocked out the sky. There wasn't much ground cover, and we moved quickly and silently as I searched the forest's spongy floor and fallen nurse logs for man tracks and booby traps. A raven's cry broke the silence. It was far away and echoed over the thickening mist and the increasingly louder roar of the creek's rapids. It wasn't long before we picked up an animal trail that wound down the hill at right angles toward our direction. I paused and studied the tracks: cougar, deer, and elk, all heading for the creek.

Jamie bent over with her hands on her knees and said, "The creek flows into a large pool. That's why it attracts so many animals. Let's follow it. Animals always take the easy way, and we've got to go that way before we start the climb to Bear Chief's and Bear Mother's cave."

I scanned left and right. "Sometimes, the easy way kills," I said. "It's best to stay off trails. Can't we reach the cave by pushing up to our right?"

"Yes, but wouldn't it—"

"Too easy to walk into an ambush," I interrupted. "It happened too often in Nam."

"This isn't Vietnam, David."

"Jonathan doesn't know that," I whispered. "No more talk."

The clouds parted for a moment and sunlight lit a flash of light across the animal trail. I dropped to my knees as I pulled Jamie down.

"What's the matter?" she puffed as her chest hit the ground.

She tried to rise up, but I held her down and ordered, "Shut up and stay down. Your brother's been here. Hell, he could still be here. Stay put and stay quiet. If anything happens—and I mean anything, hightail it out of here and don't look back."

I slid forward on my belly with the Winchester off safety toward a Douglas fir on the right side of the flash of light. When I reached the base of the tree, I slowly cleared debris from its roots and traced both hands up the trunk. When I found what I was looking for, disconnected it, and motioned to Jamie.

"What's that" she asked when I showed her what I found. "A hand grenade?"

"It sure is." I pointed to the firing mechanism. "Look, the detonator's missing. The damned thing's a dud." I showed her the wire and yanked hard. She watched it vibrate ankle high across the trail to where it was tied to a second Douglas fir. "This trip wire was tied to the grenade. Anyone walking by trips the wire, pops the pin, and kisses his life goodbye. Simple and effective."

"But why a dud?"

"My guess is to see if I've let down. Jonathan was warning us not to go any further. Jonathan knew we would come this way." I paused and took a deep breath. "He doesn't want to kill us, but he'll try if we go any further." I tossed the dud into the brush. "For sure, he's got the firepower. A hell of a lot more than we have."

"This is some kind of game to him," she exclaimed.

"You, of all people, should know that," I said.

"How's that?" she asked.

"Don't your people think everything's a game? Raven's game?"

She nodded her head. "I suppose so. I just never thought the proof would be so honest-to-God hard."

"We should go back and leave your brother to his own end," I said. "Hell, he deserves what's coming to him."

"How can you be so sure about what will happen?"

"I'm not sure about what will happen. I just know Jonathan isn't coming out of this in one piece. But following him will be very dangerous. If you want to go back, we will. I don't want you going back alone because Jonathan could have doubled back behind us."

"You mean he's been trailing us?"

"A distinct possibility. He's an accomplished hunter of human beings."

Jamie shook her head, "You know why we can't go back." We started walking. "We'll keep going north," she said. "We'll hit the east bank of the creek soon and follow it through the canyon until we cut up the mountain."

"Remember," I instructed again, "silence is our only friend now. We've got to stay quick and frosty without being reckless. We have to be as quiet as death itself. You've never hunted men, so do as I do when I do it."

Habits I learned in combat took over and wore on my mind, irritating and hot. My patterns of movement changed, and Jamie imitated them as best she could. We headed fast to the creek's sound, but silently, careful not to kick branches and pebbles or skid our boots over wet ground. We reached the creek about a half-hour later. It ran through a deep glacial cut between two mountains and carried rain and snow runoff to the Unuk River ten miles to the northwest. It ran fast and loud down a ten-degree slope, and the pop of small rocks pushed into the boulders by the current sounded like small arms fire. We stopped and caught our breath before we ducked behind a line of alder and brush lining the creek and started to climb. By late afternoon, under dark and rainy skies, we reached a wide outcrop. Jamie tapped my shoulders and whispered, "That's the cave straight ahead."

I nodded and replied, "The brush is too thick. Where?"

She pointed to a line of fir trees just below the gray clouds that covered the mountain's summit. "Behind that line of trees. We're on sacred ground," she said in a hushed voice I barely heard. "That's bear Chief's and Bear Mother's cave. My people were born there."

My eyes finally adjusted, and I saw the cave's opening. "If Jonathan's there, we're in for a lot of trouble. He'll have the high ground."

"The only way to know is to go look," Jamie whispered. "I don't feel him, though. I've always been able to when he's close."

"Let's get this done," I said as I took her hand and gently squeezed. "Stay close enough to whisper, back enough to get out of the way if I walk into anything."

"You're the boss here."

I released her hand and said, "Here we go."

The rain eased to a drizzle behind a soft westerly wind, and the forest came alive with movement. Movement in a rain forest is most often felt before the cause is seen, so I zeroed in on movement not pushed by the wind, movement picked up as a feeling in the belly or a chill in the spine. Twice as we climbed, I nearly hit the ground expecting the rake of gun fire. I watched for signs of Jonathan and worried about Jamie. Survival born in combat calmed my body as my emotions ebbed and flowed with the wind. I also kept checking on Jamie as we climbed, gripped by an old madness with its own sanity. I kept picking up movement I couldn't account for, movement unpushed by wind and not seen by the eye.

"You feel it too," Jamie panted as she pulled up next to me.

We crouched behind a Douglas fir. "It's nothing like I've ever felt."

"It's the ancestors," she whispered.

"You mean Haida ghost stuff?"

She took a deep breath and exhaled. "More real than ghosts, my love. More real than we are, and they've come for Jonathan."

It was too late for questions, even though I had plenty. "If what you say is true, Jonathan must be in the cave." I glanced at my watch. "It'll be dark soon. We've got to move."

She tugged at my left arm. "Aren't you afraid of the ancestors?"

"I'm crazy, not stupid," I replied. "Maybe Haida spirits and ancestors live here, maybe not. Of course I'm afraid . . . no, scared like I've never been scared before, even in Nam. I'm mostly scared of Jonathan. I know he's real. But I haven't picked up his sign since that dud grenade."

"I know he's here," Jamie whispered as she pulled closer.

"But where?" I demanded impatiently.

She ignored my frustration. "What do we do now?"

I checked my watch again and said, "We go to the cave, slow and easy," I said as I stood and helped Jamie to her feet. "Unlock that .45," I whispered.

She did as I clicked off my Winchester's safety. "Let's go," I said and motioned her to follow.

As the slope gradually leveled, the clouds in the strip of sky overhead parted into parallel red bands separated by gray clods above a wet land of increasing wind gusts and gathering darkness. As we slowly inched up, a greenish light flashed on and off on our right.

"You see that?" I whispered to Jamie.

"I see it," she gasped. The light was as quick and deft as an owl on the hunt as it flew into the cave.

"Come on," I said. "We've got to get to the cave before dark."

Twenty minutes later, we stopped at the edge of a crescent shaped flat piece of land lined with red cedars towering into decaying daylight. The flat was about fifty yards across at its widest and butted directly against the mountain. The cave's mouth seemed to yawn wide where the flat met the mountain's uprise. I scanned for traps and for signs of Jonathan.

"You still feel it?" I whispered as I unslung my backpack and crouched down.

Jamie dropped to her knees beside me. "Like you said, a dead man could feel it."

The only word I can think of to label this feeling is "power." An energy flowed from the cave and hovered over the flat. It felt serene and tranquil, as if nothing bad could enter the cave.

"Don't be fooled," Jamie warned. "This place is sacred. The peace you feel can change into something powerful and dangerous in the wink of an eye." Her face looked like a pale mask in the dusk light. "The power you feel created everything," she said. "But it gets fancy on revenge. It controls everything: ravens and bats, owls and eagles, wolves and bears, and it's waiting for us."

"Look," I said as I pointed to three evenly spaced dirt mounds several feet from the cave's mouth. "For sure, Jonathan's in the cave. Keep low." Tranquility seemed to drain from the forest like the undertow of an outgoing tide, and in place of peace, there was violation and war.

Jamie sensed the power shift. "Do you see Jonathan?"

"Just those three dirt mounds. He did a lousy job building them. The bastard's also set out claymore mines. That means he's close. Probably in the cave."

"How come he didn't hide them?" Jamie whispered.

"They aren't meant for us. My guess is he's waiting in the cave for the bears."

Jamie rose to her knees. "We've got to find out," she said.

"There's only one way," I said. I motioned her to stay down as I called out to the cave: "Jonathan, it's David. Jamie's with me. Let's talk."

There was no answer. Then the energy in the cave seemed to strengthen and pulsate at a higher frequency. "Stay behind a tree," I ordered Jamie.

She buried her face in her hands. And moaned, "Oh no! It's too late."

"What the hell are you talking about? If he's there that means the bears aren't. Damn it, there's still time!"

"You still don't understand," she sobbed.

"Not only don't I understand, I wouldn't have given up if I did," I replied angrily. Then I shouted toward the cave's entrance. "Come on, man. It's getting cold. Let's build a fire, cook some food, and get some sleep. In the morning, we'll hightail it out of here and get drunk at your grandfather's cabin." I paused and listened, and then said, "We know you're in there, man. What do you say?"

I waited for a reply, and then rolled to my left. It was an instinct, and it was just in time. Automatic rifle fire cracked blue points of lights toward my direction and as the rounds cut into the dirt where I had been crouched, I checked for Jamie and saw she wasn't hurt. "Sweet Jesus, stay low." I called to her.

Then Jonathan shouted from the cave. "I told you not to follow me!" He fired again until his clip was empty. I sighted my Winchester at Jonathan's rifle flashes and squeezed off four quick rounds.

"I told you it was too late," Jamie cried.

"It's going to be hell prying him out of that damned cave," I said.

"Weren't you listening?" she shouted angrily. "Didn't you see them? Jonathan can't come out!"

"There's no time for this," I shouted back. "Get hold of yourself. There are no bears in that cave. Just your crazy brother. And he's trying to kill us. If there were bears in that cave, Jonathan wouldn't be there." I aimed at the cave and scanned for movement. "We've got to think of something fast," I whispered.

"Listen to me," Jamie pleaded. "Bear Chief and Bear Mother are forms of the Great Spirit. There not bears as you understand 'bears.' The Great Spirit takes the form of Bear Chief and Bear Mother and Raven for my people so we can know our ancestors. Other people know other forms of the Great Spirit."

"This is no time for theology," I shouted. But I couldn't choke back the thought from my own religious way: God in the image of man. I pressed my head on the Winchester's butt for a moment, then looked up just in time to see new movement inside the cave.

Jamie saw it too. "They're in there," she exclaimed.

"Who's in there?" I shouted.

"Bear Chief and Bear Mother."

We watched movement transform into fragmented white light. Its wavelength rose and fell like breathing. The whiteness was not like a flicker of light, but more like the absence of darkness that came in sharp bursts from inside the cave. That's when the voices started. At first, I thought it was the wind. The voices sounded like disjointed babel in a crowded room, and I understood that it came from the light in the cave. Then I heard my own voice tremble incoherently, in grief, fear, and terrible understanding. "No, man, no. Oh my God," I called out. "Jonathan, you crazy bastard, my friend and my brother, they're here. Damn it, if I could, I'd kill you right now and save you the misery. There're things no one should suffer.

"I can't stand it," I cried out to Jamie, who was stretched flat on the ground, scratching the dirt with her fingers.

"Man, get out of there," I shouted to Jonathan again.

"He can't!" Jamie cried. There was something peculiar and cruel in the sound of her voice, and angry sorrow that blended with the voices in the cave. The voices wove together yet were as individually distinct as threads on a spider's web.

We finally saw Jonathan. He stood with his body backlighted like a shadow puppet. His right arm arched back and snapped forward.

"Get down," I yelled as the grenade bounced once and landed five yards in front of us and exploded. Water and mud sprayed like a geyser as the sharp whistle of M-16 fire passed overhead and sawed the limbs of trees and brush. I fired once at the shadow and then rolled to my left. I heard Jamie snap off two quick rounds with the .45. "She can do it," I thought. "Stay low behind the tree," I shouted. "He can't hit what he can't see."

Jonathan fired again, but this time into the light at the back of the cave, which had split in two. "Goddamn it, stay away!" he screamed hysterically. "Stay away! Stay away!" They were the screams of a man in combat fighting for his life and knowing he was about to die. He took aim at the light shapes again and pulled the trigger. His rifle flashed and exploded.

I jumped up and ran toward the cave as Jamie cried out, "No, don't go in!" I ignored her as I ran, not bothering to zigzag or keeping low, straight to the cave, firing my Winchester until it was empty. I heard Jonathan' moans as I closed in and found him lying on his right side. He saw me and tried to pull up to his knees and crawl away. I dropped my Winchester and kneeled. I gently turned him on his back as I checked for wounds. There were no bullet injuries, but his legs were bent at the wrong angle and there was heavy bleeding where his leg bones were crushed just above both knees. His face was a mess of charred flesh and dried blood. I understood why when I saw his M-16. He had rested the muzzle in the dirt and stopped up the barrel as he reloaded. When he fired at Jamie and me again, his M-16 exploded and tore away half his face.

I found the claymore detonator and yanked the wires. "Aw man," I uttered, "you've run out of time." Jonathan groaned again as he clawed at the dirt with his left hand. "The only time you have left is now." I looked away toward the sound of running feet approaching the cave's mouth.

"Mother of Jesus," Jamie cried when she saw Jonathan.

"Is the .45 empty?" I asked.

Jamie kneeled beside Jonathan as she handed me the .45. "I don't know," she replied breathlessly. "Can we get him out of here? He's hurt bad."

"Wait outside," I said as I looked into Jonathan's terrified eyes as I checked the .45. "One round left," I whispered. "Do you want it, man?"

Jamie stared at me, then Jonathan, then at me again, and finally at the two shadows gently pulsing at the back of the cave. "What are you going to do?" she asked.

"What you brought me here to do," I snapped. "Now, get out and wait."

The light in the cave dimmed to gray as deep growls rumbled from the cave's interior. "Behind you," Jamie cried. "Behind you, behind you, behind you!"

"I know," I said with a sense of calmness that flowed through me and over me. "You can't do anything here, my love. Now please go."

Jamie slowly rose to her feet as she fixed her gaze on the two dark shadows. The growling grew louder as she backed out of the cave, and then turned into the belly rumbles of two large bears. She didn't take her eyes off the shadows until she was clear of the cave.

Jonathan saw the shapes and heard the sounds too, and his eyes turned red in terror. "You've finally seen them, haven't you? You bloody bastard," I snapped. "You've always believed in them. Why haven't you seen them before now?" He started to hyperventilate and scream, but all he could manage was to grasp for air.

"I don't know why I'm doing this," I said to him as I turned and looked at the two forms and saw what Jonathan saw—a boar and sow grizzly gently swaying from side to side on all fours. "No man deserves this," I shouted to the two bears. "No even this man."

Then I focused on Jonathan again and aimed the .45 between his eyes. The bear's growls intensified as Jonathan suffered a last burst of frenzied energy. I screamed and fired. Jonathan's head snapped backwards with both his eyes wide open in circles of dread. I ran from the cave without looking back. I found Jamie sitting in some grass and spoke to her. She didn't answer at first, and when she did, her only words were, "He's dead." Her voice was calm and reconciled and reminded me of the sound of voices after combat, how men asked and answered questions to assure one another that the perimeter was secured.

She started to cry. "It was hard. For you and Jonathan."

"It's no longer hard for Jonathan," I said as I surrounded her in my arms. "But we will carry this until death frees us as it did him."

"Is this what hell feels like?" she asked.

"For us, yes."

19

It was too dark to return to Raven's House, so we spent the night in the forest without sleep or conversation. Wind pushed hard through the trees, but by morning softened and seemed to settle tranquilly over the land and the numbing resignation of our souls. At first light, we hauled out for Raven's House, and by late morning, as the sun threw bright light on the land, we found Born of Songs working on his totem pole.

"Jonathan's dead, Born of Songs," I said.

Born of Songs nodded and continued carving on the pole. His movements were labored and told me he neither required nor wanted details.

"It's sad he went crazy," I said.

"My grandson was one of those the Great Spirit didn't finish."

I watched Jamie trace her hands over the totem's newest carving. "You have seen what's in the cedar, Grandfather."

"I have seen," Born of Songs answered. "Raven sent Owl to call my name in the night. That's when I saw what's in this log. I must finish soon." He paused and smiled. "How come we have these bodies? They are too weak to carry what we feel. Sometimes I get so hemmed in by my arms and legs I look forward to getting past them. Death will set me as free as a cloud in the wind."

I dropped my backpack. "Is Jonathan Blue Heron free as a cloud?"

"Look at what I carved and see for yourself," he answered as he tapped the pole with his chisel. "It is it good to remember how someone died. It's the one lonely act in his life. In all other things, even our birth, we are bound to others. But the time of dying is our own."

I looked at the unfinished carvings on the pole. "What do you see, my son?" Born of Songs asked.

"You're my teacher in these things. What should I see?"

"Help David see, Bear Mother's Daughter," Born of Songs instructed.

Jamie pointed to each carving. "Here, a boar and a sow grizzly on all fours with a man standing, one foot on each back. A bird with spread wings pulls the man's head up with its talons. This is Raven."

"And they shall mount up with the wings of eagles," I whispered.

"What's that?" Born of Songs asked.

"Nothing," I replied. "Just something my people sometimes say. It's from the Bible."

"Life can't be cut off so quick," Jamie continued. "No one is dead until the things they've changed are dead. The things Jonathan changed—good and bad—are traces of his life. As long as someone remembers, he won't be cut off because he's dead."

"That's why I must finish this pole," Born of Songs said sadly as he began carving. "You are both so young. Someday you will know how life runs down and stops, how it is to use all your power just to get up in the morning,"

"Let us help, Grandfather," Jamie said.

"There is sorrow in your words," Born of Songs said to both of us as he continued carving. "That's good. Where there is sorrow there is love. Love is the pain of life. Where there is pain, there is love and life. So, find life together."

"We will, Born of Songs, we will," I said. "But first I must go back to the cave. There's something I've got to do."

Jamie shuttered and said, "I don't know why, but if you must, I'm going with you."

"I know the way now. Stay with Born of Songs." I picked up my backpack and Winchester. "We'll spend the night at Raven's House. I'll take off in the morning and be back before dark."

"There's no need, my son" Born of Songs said.

"I have a need," I replied in a strong voice that surprised me. "I won't leave him there rotting on the cave floor. He needs to be buried. I owe him that."

"What needs doing has already been done," Born of Songs gently replied. "There's nothing left to do."

"I won't leave him like that," I repeated angrily. "I'm going back to dig a hole and bury him."

"They will take care of him," Jamie joined in. "You don't have to—"

I cut her off. "They?" I snapped. "Bear Chief, Bear Mother, Raven?" I stared at both of them trough damp eyes. "I'm going alone," I said once more.

After Jamie and I returned to Raven's House, Born of Songs continued working through the night by the light of a campfire while I slept throughout the night beside Jamie, a hard sleep without dreams until the hunting sounds of a bald eagle brought me to consciousness. For a while, I lay on my back and listened to the eagle cries and Jamie's soft breathing. When I felt fully awakened, I stood, picked up my backpack, and crept outside.

I waited for a moment in the campfire's light and studied Born of Song's progress. Raven was now clearly formed at the pole's crown and the other figures would soon be completed. "It's almost finished, Grandfather," I said as I hoisted my backpack to my shoulders.

"You called me "Grandfather?'"

"It seems appropriate now."

Born of Songs nodded and continued to work. "Where is our rifle?" he asked.

"Don't need it. Do you have a shovel?"

He brushed and blew wood chips from the place he carved. "There's an old Army surplus trench shovel leaning next to the door. I thought you'd want it, so I left it for you."

It was next to my right leg, and I picked it up. "Thanks," I said as I headed toward the trail. "Be back before dark."

Born of Songs ignored me and focused on the Raven's left eye as he fine carved with a sharp straight nosed chisel. Somewhere in the mountains behind Raven's House, a lone bull elk trumpeted so loud that an echo answered him as it were another bull elk. It's a rare day when rain does not track over these mountains. When I reached the cave, I thought I would find Jonathan's body the way I left it. But all that was left was a stripped clean skeleton of what used to be Jonathan Blue Heron hanging arms outstretched from a pole and crossbeam stuck into the cave's floor. A single bear claw hung from the skeleton's neck and a piece of Jonathan's leg bone was clamped between the skeleton's mouth. I backed away, took one last look, and walked away from the cave. By the time I got to the river and picked up the trail to Raven's House, I finally knew the truth with a dispassionate interest of an observer on the outside looking in. By late afternoon, as I entered the clearing and saw totem pole stabbing the gray sky, and I understood with equal dispassion what I had to do.

Later that night we sat by the fire in Raven's House. Our talk was short with little place for tears. What could we do? Scream? Mourn? Go mad? All of this was tried many times before Jonathan's ancestors took him. As for me, I no longer had the energy to ask the unanswerable question: why was I chosen to end my friend's life? Now Born of Songs laid on his side weary from work and age and loss, finally asleep, as Jamie and I talked about our future.

"What now?" she asked.

I smiled and replied, "I might ask you the same question."

"What's so damned funny?" she snapped.

"Sorry, it's not you. I'm laughing at myself. After all that's happened, only one thing seems certain. You and I can't go back to the way things were. Everything's definitely too changed for that. I guess I'll drive to Prince Rupert early in the morning."

"I'll go with you," Jamie replied.

"No," I said. "Stay with Grandfather. He's very weak and he needs you."

"You're right," she answered dejectedly. "He's very tired. He will leave this world soon. I don't want to believe it even though I know it is true."

"Don't be sad, my love. Born of Song's isn't. He knows his life is nearly done. He's ready to go to the ancestors."

"When will you return," she asked.

"Some time day after tomorrow. I've got to call the university in Seattle, but there's no phone here. I've got to tell my colleagues that I won't be returning to Seattle and that I'm mailing my resignation to the university's provost."

"David, are you sure that's wise?"

"I have no idea what wisdom is. All I know for sure is that I killed my best friend and that there's sure as hell nothing for us in Seattle."

"For us?" Jamie asked. "What do you mean?"

"Can you go back to the way things were? After everything that's happened?"

"That doesn't mean I know where I'm going either."

"Try trusting the Haida Way," I said. "A journey begins with the first step."

"Then it's true," she whispered. "You have come into my world. The only trouble is, the Haida Way isn't my only path now. You've seen to that."

"That's payback, my love."

Her eyes brightened. "Payback for what?" she asked softly.

"The white man's way isn't my only path anymore. You and Born of Songs have seen to that."

"Don't forget Raven and Bear Mother."

"I haven't."

"So now what?" Jamie asked as she drew her head into my chest.

"I guess we'll both have to figure out where this journey ends."

"What about Jonathan?"

"What about him? He's with the ancestors. The immediate problem is, it won't be long before Grandfather dies. He'll need our help to finish the pole."

"My people in Ketchikan will help if we ask. Will they be surprised to see you."

"Not as surprised as I am. But Born of Song's breathing is very slow and shallow. He doesn't have much time."

"Oh David!" Jamie exclaimed as she started to cry. "We've got to figure out how to live with this."

"I have a hunch that we will. But I know this much for certain. Some day I'll go back to the cave. I will get Jonathan's bones and put them in the burial pole with Born of Songs."

"Maybe someday we'll understand it all," she said.

The tone of her voice set me back. I had heard this tone before, but never so loving and intimate and strong. It is the strength of hope because we are together absolutely, and she absolutely trusts me, and nothing can separate us. I drew her down beside me. My arms encircled her waist, and the steady pressure of her arching back pushed her chest into mine. I love it this way. The shape of her head in the glowing fire light, her black hair lacing down her back, her graceful form beside me, and her strength flowing inside me. Was it all a dream? Maybe we had dreamed and were only now waking up. Everything seemed misty and a whole lifetime has passed us by. Yet out of the mist, something new might be reborn.

It is the spirit of all of us. It is Jonathan Blue Heron's spirit, crazy drunk and crazy sober, fighting to be someone he couldn't be, sacrificed by the spirits he hated. It is Nathan Born of Songs spirit, filled with Haida history and culture, now about to soar to his ancestors. It is Jamie Bear Mother's Daughter's spirit, singing the songs of her people, suffering no fools lightly. It is the spirit of illusion, the spirit mind of music that rises above lyrics, the spirit of truth behind concepts. It is Raven's spirit that takes on whatever shapes people give it. It is a trickster's spirit that is always present, creative and destructive, according to its own rhythms. For the Haida, its forms are Raven and Bear Mother, and the ancestors. It is what white people call "God."

And I have a premonition. It will not come true this year, nor the next. But it will come true. I will tap someone on the shoulder and do some explaining. Whoever it is will listen to me while Jamie sings of Bear Chief and Bear Mother. I will build up a fire and tell Raven's and Jonathan's story, and maybe carve a new totem pole.